THE LITTLE GIRL I ALWAYS WANTED

A totally addictive psychological thriller
with a shocking twist

ANYA MORA

Joffe Books, London
www.joffebooks.com

First published in Great Britain in 2023

Cover art by Nick Castle

ISBN: 978-1-83526-280-1

CHAPTER 1

Jubilee

They're talking about me.

I needed to go to the bathroom, so I left my bedroom, and tiptoed down the hall, and heard them.

Now, back in my room, it's impossible to forget their words, even though I cover my ears with my hands, even though I bury my face in the pillow, even though I squeeze my eyes shut and try to go to a far, far-away place, it's impossible.

I know why they're upset. Why they are crying. It's because of me. If I had never been brought here, if I had never joined this family, it wouldn't be like this. They would still be happy with all of their perfect kids, and I wouldn't have messed it all up.

When my social worker told me I was going to be adopted and have a forever family, it was like a dream come true. I'd been waiting for that moment for five years, ever since I was four years old and brought into foster care. I'd been hoping, crossing my fingers, saying a prayer every single night, that one day someone would want me enough to love me forever.

And I thought that was Annie and David. They said I could call them Mom and Dad, but real Moms and Dads don't talk like that, do they? My foster mom shouted, but that is different. She was paid to take care of me.

"She should never have come here."

"I understand, Annie. But what are we gonna do now? She is already here."

You don't say that about your kids, do you? Well, I guess some do. My mom did. My dad did too. Not that I can hardly remember either of them. The last time I saw them, I was four years old, and no one came to pick me up from my friend Lucia's birthday party at Chuck E. Cheese. They brought me there even though I didn't have a gift in hand, and they told Lucia's family that they'd be back in a few hours to pick me up. They never came.

Eventually, Lucia's mom called the police, and they took me away. And I remember thinking, that party — where Lucia got so many presents from so many people — was one of the last things that ever happened to me before my world fell apart. Lucia was treated like a princess that day. But then Mom and Dad were gone forever, and I started living in a bunch of different foster homes, one after the other, until finally, I had a family who wanted to adopt me. Keep me theirs forever.

I thought it was going to be perfect. When they brought me here to their big house, I thought my life was finally going to turn around. I was finally going to be a princess in a fairytale with a happily ever after. Suddenly I had five older siblings who wanted to take care of me and talk to me and do fun things with me. I even got a grandma and grandpa who lived in the house behind ours, and I thought, *That is what a real family is like. Everyone together laughing and playing games and having big family dinners.*

But now Annie and David are upset, and it is all because of me.

I'm the reason families break up. Maybe I wasn't good enough, and that's why my first mom and dad never came back to Lucia's party to get me, and maybe that's why Annie and David are talking about wanting me gone, now. Maybe

I'm the problem. I close my eyes, wishing it wasn't the truth, wishing I wasn't such a messed-up little girl. When things got bad at my foster home, I would run away. For a little while, when I was alone hiding somewhere, I would feel safer than I ever had before.

I want to feel that way again.

I can't stay here any longer and keep ruining their lives. Annie and David deserve more than that.

They deserve to be happy, not be stuck with a kid that they don't want. I blink back the tears in my bedroom, and I sit up from my bed — the bed that has a pink bedspread and pink pillows and a white blanket that's fuzzy like a lamb. I never deserve to have all these nice things. They're too perfect for a girl like me.

You'd think in nine years, I would've figured out how to be the sort of girl that parents like, but I haven't. I watched the other girls in the foster homes, watched how they acted, how they smiled or said *yes, please,* and how they got along with the other kids to make the foster parents happy. I tried to pay attention so that I could be a girl like that, too. A girl who did everything right.

Something inside me must be messed up because I don't always say *thank you,* and I don't always say *please.* And sometimes I forget to wash my hands before dinner, and I'm not that great at reading or math.

I do love animals, which is one of the reasons I loved moving here. The farm has so many cute pets. My favorite thing is feeding the chickens and collecting their eggs.

But I'm not going to do that anymore, because this isn't where I belong. And this family is already so perfect, I don't want to be the one to ruin everything for them.

I take my backpack, the blue one that Annie picked out for me, and I shove in a blanket and a drawing pad and some pencils. From the corner behind my mattress, I pull out the granola bars I've stashed there, which I know isn't right, but it's hard for me not to hide food all over my room. It's like my mind remembers not having enough, of fighting for my share at the foster homes, and now I'm scared of that ever happening again. I grab some juice boxes from the back of my closet and shove them in the backpack, too, along with the candy bars that Emily bought me when we went shopping last week.

I put on my coat and my rain boots, and then I slide open the bedroom window. I'm glad I'm on the first floor. It makes it easier to climb out the window.

When my feet hit the grass, I look back at the house just for a second, wondering if I'm making the right decision. Maybe I should go talk to David and Annie, tell them that I'm sorry for messing everything up. They aren't shouting anymore. The house is quiet.

But I don't turn back. I don't want to be in the way. Not anymore, not ever again.

I cross through the yard, cut through the far pasture until I reach the tree line. I enter the woods, where the trees get crowded. I keep weaving through them, not completely sure of where I'm going to go but remembering there's a treehouse about a half a mile away that Mason showed me once. Annie said it's too far for me to go there alone. She didn't want me to get lost. But right now, I feel like I never want to be found.

I can get there and hide out until I figure out where to go next.

I begin to run through the woods when I hear something snap in the distance. I stop in my tracks, wanting to call out, wishing I had a flashlight, something to guide me besides the full moon that hangs heavy in the sky.

But there's nothing out here. It's just me.

Another branch cracks.

Well, me and someone else.

"Hello?" I say. And I'm frightened like I've never been before.

CHAPTER 2

I look over at my husband, David, and squeeze his hand. He's driving our big twelve-passenger van and although there are only three of us in the vehicle at the moment, it feels so much more full than that. It is because there is an overflow of love. My prayers have been answered.

It's as if my heart is bursting out of my chest. I turn around in my seat, looking at the little girl sitting behind me. She's beaming, which makes me beam, which in turn makes David grin.

"You girls haven't had that smile off your faces in over an hour," he says.

I laugh. "It's just pretty exciting, isn't it, Jubilee?"

Our new nine-year-old daughter nods. "I'm so excited to see the house."

The adoption isn't final. As a foster adoption, it will take several months to process the paperwork, but the agency we worked with to bring her home assured us everything is in motion. Now, all we need is patience and love.

"And we're so excited to show it to you," I tell her. We'd met just one time before we went to a putt-putt golf course in Olympia, where she's from. We didn't bring the other kids with us, not wanting to overwhelm Jubilee. We probably made the right call. David and I were able to get to know Jubilee, fall in love with her, and make a commitment to be her parents forever.

"And you have chickens, right?" Jubilee asks.

David chuckles. "Yeah, I think we got about three dozen of them, so I hope you like eggs."

"I love eggs," she says. "I like them scrambled or fried or hard-boiled."

"Are you pretty easygoing about most food?" I ask.

She shrugs. "I'm not so picky."

"All right, well, I can't wait to learn your favorites," I tell her, meaning it.

Her brown eyes sparkle, and her thick black hair hangs to her waist. She has long eyelashes and skin that glistens like sand. She is petite but sturdy. I know that because when she wrapped her arms around me in a hug this morning, I felt her strength. I hope she can harness it, take all the pain that she has experienced and turn it into something brave and beautiful.

The fact I get to be a part of any of that journey feels like an honor. I look at her and see her eyes shine with emotion.

"You doing okay?" I ask Jubilee.

"I'm great. Why?"

"I just imagine it's a lot," I tell her. We're almost home. "I just want to make sure that you're doing all right before we get there. The house can be loud. There are five siblings for you to meet a — well, four are at home. Elijah is in the Army, remember? And he couldn't get leave. Plus Grandma and Grandpa. I just don't want to overwhelm you."

"I'll be okay," she says. "I'm excited."

I believe her. I can feel her excitement bubbling out and it helps calm my worries. Even though I am the one who instigated this whole decision of going through the adoption process and bringing home a child, I haven't always been one hundred percent certain it was the right choice.

I know it's going to change a lot of things for our family. Our youngest, Jonas, is fourteen years old, and the other four kids are stair-stepped right above him.

Choosing to have a nine-year-old daughter join our family means it will be five additional years before David and I are empty nesters. But I love being a mom, having a big family, a house full of noise and laughter and food. The idea of all of that ending in a few years when Mason graduates is hard to handle.

More than hard to handle. It feels impossible to imagine.

I'll just keep finding ways to grow my family so I can prolong my role as a stay-at-home mom just a little bit longer. I'm thankful to be supported by David to stay home with the children. It was always my dream. My own childhood had been chaotic. My parents had a heated divorce and were never on speaking terms. There wasn't a sense of security or stability . . . and I wanted to provide the opposite of that for my own family. And I wanted these years with kids in the house to be extended . . . the idea of not having a child at home to take care of was the catalyst for the adoption.

And yes, I know I will always be a mom, but when the kids are gone, it changes. I know that enough with Elijah leaving for the military. And Emily will be gone in six months, once she and Jaden get married.

Emily has been my only daughter until today. And she has been my right-hand person in the kitchen and at home. Not having her as a part of my daily life will be so different. I'm not saying I'm replacing Emily with Jubilee, but it does make the pain of my older daughter growing up a little less severe.

When I tried to talk to my best friend Susannah about this, she didn't understand. She has one son and seems perfectly content. My mother-in-law, Sarah, has more sympathy. She always wanted more children than David, but she had uterine cancer shortly after David was born, which ruled out more biological children. She says she always regrets not adopting — that her heart always longed for a bigger family.

My other dear friend, Lisa, is the same age as me, and her family continues to grow. She has eight children now, and she and her husband John, are of the belief that each child is another blessing from God, which at times sounds more than trite. Their daughter Leah has been missing for three months, and I am unclear on what God has to do with that.

Belfair, where we live, is about an hour and fifteen minutes from Olympia, out on the peninsula. As we drive toward town, I begin seeing missing person signs. They're on the posts throughout town.

Seeing the signs always sends a deep pain through me. I have known Leah her whole life; we've gone to church together and been in the same homeschool co-op. I am heartbroken for Lisa, as she's been one of my closest friends for two decades, and the fact that her fifteen-year-old daughter is gone is horrific for everyone in the community.

It has been especially painful on Josh, my fifteen-year-old son, who has been best friends with Leah since they were toddlers.

It's only been a few months, but the posters telling people that she's missing are already frayed and should be replaced. I can remember to do that. Be a good friend to Lisa in the way she's always been such a good friend to me.

I know David registers the missing person signs, but Jubilee, in her happiness, doesn't seem to notice them, and that gives me a bit of relief. I don't want her to know that there has been heartache in the new community into which she's moving.

When we get to the house, Jubilee gasps.

Look, David and I are not millionaires. We're not rolling in cash, but we do have a beautiful property of fifty acres that has been in his family for a hundred years. We live in the big family farmhouse that, while it doesn't have all the modern amenities of a new build, certainly has plenty of character. A big front porch, plenty of bedrooms, and a deep cast iron kitchen sink that can hold all the dishes from a family-style dinner.

David's parents, James and Sarah, live behind us in a much smaller two-bedroom home that was at one point the living quarters for the hired help. Twenty-one years ago, after I gave birth to our first child, Elijah, the smaller home was remodeled and they moved in. That way, David, their only child, would have plenty of room to grow his own family. We had plans for a big family, even then.

I know how incredibly lucky we are to all be so close. This property is like a cocoon from the world at large. I homeschool my kids, so I'm usually here with my mother-in-law, Sarah, keeping the homestead together while James, my father-in-law, and David are off getting bids for new projects. When not working on maintaining the large property, David and his dad are working on new builds throughout the peninsula. They co-own a construction company, Davies Family Construction.

"Do you like it?" I ask Jubilee.

She nods. "The house looks like it belongs in a movie."

"I think you're right," I tell her, trying to see the familiar home through her childlike eyes. The daffodils of March, bright yellow in the flower beds surrounding the porch, the rose bushes sprouting the tiniest of buds, with green leaves bright as the grass, ready to emerge with fragrant petals, the rosemary bush as high as my waist that has been there for as long as I can remember.

And that is just the front of the house. "Look," I say pointing to the right, the big red barn in the distance. "Do you see the chickens pecking about?"

"They don't have to stay in a cage?" she asks.

"A cage? No," I say, "they're free range here."

David parks the van in front of the house, and I jump out of the passenger door before sliding open Jubilee's door in the back.

David goes to the back of the van to grab the few tote bins holding Jubilee's possessions.

I take Jubilee's hand. "You ready to meet the kids?"

"Of course," she says, just as our family begins piling out of the house onto the front porch.

Elijah isn't here, of course. He is stationed at Fort Hood in Texas and won't be back until Christmas.

Next up is Emily, my nineteen-year-old. She runs down the steps, wrapping Jubilee in her arms. "Oh my gosh, it's so good to meet you!" Emily's blonde hair is loosely curled, and the dress she's wearing is one she sewed herself. It's a blue-striped pattern that falls just below her knees.

Andrew has his arms crossed on the front porch. At seventeen, he's best described as angry and reckless, which is maybe the least flattering thing a mother can say about her child, but he's struggled the last year or so. It breaks my heart, but all I can do is hope he passes through this phase and becomes a stronger person, a better man.

"Andrew, come meet Jubilee," I say, urging him forward.

He takes the steps and then offers her his hand. "Good to meet you, Jubilee."

"Nice to meet you too," she says with a smile.

Josh follows. At fifteen, he is usually a pretty good-natured kid, except, of course, the last three months have been much harder on him since Leah's disappearance.

Still, the difficult things he's endured haven't turned him hard like his brother Andrew. Instead, they've made him soft and emotional, and there are tears in his eyes more often than there used to be. Lisa's daughter, Leah, was his very best friend. Her going missing has broken his heart.

And then there's Mason. He is fourteen and my baby. His hair is curly, his eyes are green as the pine trees around us, and he grins at Jubilee. "Finally," he says, "I'm not the youngest kid in the house."

Everyone chuckles at that, Jubilee especially.

When James and Sarah, my in-laws, come down the porch to greet Jubilee, they exclaim at how lovely she is and how happy they are to meet her.

Sarah wraps her in an arm and says, "I can't wait to get all your measurements, because I plan on sewing you some new clothes."

Jubilee looks down at her jeans and worn shirt. "Can I wear dresses like Emily?" she asks.

Sarah laughs. "Dresses are my specialty."

Jubilee looks up at me as if marveling that this is her new reality.

"It's true," I say. "If you can't find her, best guess is she is in her sewing room."

"Well," David says. "Do you want to go inside and see the house? See your new bedroom, just for you?"

"I get my very own bedroom?" she asks.

My kids exchange glances. Then look over at me and their dad. One simple phrase can say so much, and my children recognize this. David has a very successful business, and though we lead a simple life, we have more than enough. The kids have their own bedrooms because this farmhouse is huge, and there are plenty of bathrooms in the house as well. They've always had food that's warm and nourishing and clothes that are made or purchased with care. A dad who's around; a mom who's always at home.

They've had so much, and Jubilee has had so little.

When I show her the new bedroom, tears fill her eyes. Emily stands beside me and squeezes my hand.

"Oh, Mom," she says. "You've made her so happy."

I blink back tears as I watch Jubilee walk around her bedroom, running her hand over the pink-and-purple quilt I made myself, pointing out the blue backpack that's hanging on the hook beside her bedroom door. On the desk, there are sketch pads, coloring books and mason jars filled with pencils and crayons and markers, all lined up in a row.

Everything in the room is a wish fulfillment for a nine-year-old little girl. There are even a few American Girl dolls that Emily has passed down to her in the corner, just ready to be played with. There are four of them, and a whole dresser filled with their accessories. I know Jubilee is going to have a fun time going through all these new-to-her treasures.

And most little girls would get distracted by all this new stuff, but Jubilee instead turns around to us smiling, wiping the tears from her eyes.

"Thank you," she says, "thank you for bringing me home. Thank you for choosing me to be your family."

CHAPTER 3

Annie
Three months later

Josh looks a wreck. I'm saying that with as much motherly affection as possible. His eyes have dark shadows under them, and they're constantly rimmed in red. He's lost weight. He's not himself, and at fifteen years old, he should be growing into a strong young man like his brothers Andrew and Elijah were at this age.

I know the change in him is because of Leah going missing. It's breaking him up inside, but she's been gone for six months, and still there's no lead.

He is pouring a glass of orange juice with such a sad look on his face that I feel like I could cry. I don't want him to bring this attitude to homeschool co-op today — not because I want him to hide his emotions, but because I want him to be happy. I want him to be himself.

"Listen," I say. We're in the kitchen, where the other kids are finishing up their breakfast of yogurt and granola. "I know you're having a hard time, but there's a lot of kids at co-op who look up to you. I need you to bring your best self today."

"I'm sorry," he says. "I'm not trying to be anything besides my best. It's just been hard. I'm sorry. I really am, Mom."

He doesn't lean in for a hug. He doesn't give me a smile or the wink, the things I always used to get from him. He's withdrawn. Everyone can feel it.

"Hey, Josh," Mason says, from the table. "I got a text from Nathan. He wants to pull together a pickup soccer game after class. Sound good?"

Josh shakes his head. "I don't think I can, but—"

I cut him off. "Josh, what were we just talking about?"

"Fine," he says, "I'll be there. I'm gonna go outside. I'll meet you at the car."

"I just have a few things to get together. Your lunches, most importantly, and Jubilee, are you almost ready?" I call out my youngest daughter's name. "Jubilee?"

She bounces into the kitchen with her hair in two long braids, her smile big. I am relieved to see her in a good mood. One thing I have discovered over the last few months is that Jubilee's disposition is a rollercoaster. It is high or low, and the turns come out of nowhere. The fact that she is happy as she bounces into the kitchen means co-op day isn't going to be like a ride on Splash Mountain.

She's wearing her favorite dress that her grandma Sarah made her. She twirls around. "What do you think, Mama?"

"I think you look just lovely. Did you do those braids by yourself?"

She laughs. "I wish! Emily did 'em for me."

"She's a good big sister, isn't she?" I give Jubilee a side hug. "Now, I need you to eat your yogurt quickly. We're already running late."

She pulls out a chair and sits next to Andrew at the table. Andrew, who is usually a little grumpy this time of day manages to give her a smile and knock his elbow against hers. "Morning, squirt."

She giggles. "Squirt? You always have a new nickname for me."

Andrew grins. "Eh? You make it easy."

14

I focus on the lunch. I'm preparing ham-and-cheese sandwiches in Ziploc baggies, slices of apples, broccoli, ranch dressing, and molasses cookies for dessert. I fill everyone's water bottles and add them to my basket. With everything packed, I wrap a scarf around my neck and put my feet in my black clogs.

"All right, you guys ready?"

They quickly rinse their dishes and load them into the dishwasher, and then we all head outside toward the van. Their dad is already off to a construction site for the day.

Emily meets me in the entry. "Have a good day, Mom."

I smile at my daughter. "What are you up to, Emily?"

"I'm watching Tonya's kids this morning." Tonya is our neighbor three doors down. "And then I'm going to Brooke's parents' place. Shanice and I are working on the invitations for the wedding."

"Very exciting," I say, knowing Shanice, Jaden's mom, is really artistic, and the perfect person to help with this task. "I can't wait to see them. You both are so crafty."

"You sure you're okay with me doing that without you?"

"Of course. I'm glad that you can do that with Shanice. And she doesn't have any daughters, so I am sure she loves being included in the wedding plans. It'll be a nice way for you two to bond."

Emily's face lights up. "She is easy to get along with. I feel so lucky. I love my future in-laws."

"I know you do," I say, "And we are both fortunate in that." My in-laws, James and Sarah, have been a huge blessing in my life.

Emily waves goodbye to Jubilee, who is the last to leave the house. "Have a great day at co-op, Juju."

But that stops Jubilee from walking down the porch steps. Her big brown eyes become a puddle of tears instantly. This is nothing new. Jubilee is quick to reveal her emptions — something we have all become increasingly aware of. Sometimes it is ecstasy, overflowing with excitement. Sometimes it is anger, where she stomps her feet and shouts.

Sometimes it is the waterworks. Maybe we are riding Splash Mountain today, after all.

"No," she sobs, wrapping her arms around Emily's waist. "I want Emily to come with us."

"I can't, sweetie," Emily says calmly, her eyes meeting mine in a silent plea. Emily is great with Jubilee, but sometimes the intensity of Juju is a lot for anyone. "I am babysitting for the neighbors."

Jubilee starts stomping her feet on the driveway. "No, I want to go with you to Tonya's house."

I exhale, wanting to end this tantrum as quick as possible. Jubilee is very good at escalating things. "Look, you love co-op. You have an art lesson today."

Her shoulders heave as she collects herself, remembering how much she likes the art projects.

"We're going to have a great day," I assure her, hoping it's true. With Josh on the edge over Leah, Andrew's perpetual teen angst and Jubilee's propensity toward melodrama, I hope my words will prove true.

Once everyone's buckled up and the doors are shut, I look in the rearview mirror. In the back are Jubilee, Josh and Mason. Andrew is next to me in the passenger seat.

"Thanks for getting out of the house in one piece," I tell them. They smile, rolling their eyes as if there was an alternative. Order is the backbone of our family, and as much as I wish I were a free spirit at heart, I crave routine. My childhood was anything but — and I always wanted my kids to have stability over everything else. I would do anything to give it to them — in fact, I have. I have given my whole life to being their mother.

CHAPTER 4

Leah
Six months earlier

I always thought I would have my first kiss on my Sweet Sixteen. Maybe that's old-fashioned, to want to wait so long for that moment, but here I am now, in the backyard with Josh, on my fifteenth birthday.

And gosh, do I want him to kiss me.

Both of our families are inside, probably cleaning up dishes and getting stuff out for cake and ice cream. And even though I'm supposed to be the center of attention, we both come from big enough families that it's pretty easy to slip between the cracks and disappear.

That's how we first became friends all those years ago. We were three years old, and our moms were in the kitchen drinking coffee and talking about something — probably potty training or meal planning — and we slipped downstairs, past the playroom, and I showed him my favorite hiding space. It was this tiny closet underneath the stairwell where all these old boxes of Christmas ornaments were stored. I pressed my pointer finger to my lips, warning him we needed to be quiet. Not that we really needed to be *so* quiet. Even back then, no one was looking for us. Our moms certainly weren't. They had enough other children to worry about. Both of them were caring for newborns and probably already pregnant once again.

Anyway, no one found us for hours, and eventually, we took a nap. The story goes that at some point the moms realized their toddlers were missing and made a frantic search to find us. They found us fast asleep.

Josh has four siblings, but I have seven. We're both just one of many, and I always think it's crazy how our moms just want more.

"You really think your parents are going to go through with an adoption?" I ask him. We're sitting on the swing side by side, a playground I haven't been on in years. It's dark out. The stars are bright. I don't feel fifteen. I suddenly feel a lot older than that, and when I look over at Josh, it's like I see tears in his eyes, but I don't know why.

"What is it?" I ask.

He shrugs, his feet finding the ground as his swing slows to a stop. "I don't know why my mom wants another kid. It's like she's not satisfied with what she has. It's not enough. Like we're not enough."

"I don't think that's it," I say. "I mean, there are lots of kids that need families. Isn't that a good thing? The Bible tells us to take care of orphans and widows."

"Yeah," he says, "so why not take care of the widows? Why the kids? I mean, our houses are already full."

"I know," I say. "But it's really not our place to weigh in, is it?"

"No," he says. "That's why when I grow up, I'm not going to have any kids."

"Really?" I'm so surprised at this. "I always assumed I'd be a mom," I tell him.

He frowns. "Are you set on that?"

I shrug. "It's kind of what I know. I mean, you know how the church is."

He nods. "Yeah, I do."

We go to a conservative church. Most of the women wear skirts and long hair, and even though Josh's mom is a little bit more lenient than mine, I've never seen any of our parents drink alcohol, let alone say a swear word. Instead of family vacations to the ocean or something, we always go to church camp. And instead of going to the movies on the weekend, we go to youth group. We believe that the Bible is black and white, and in a lot of ways, I'm thankful for how I've been raised. I have learned to lead with compassion and understanding and grace, but sometimes I also feel like a lot of what I've learned from church is about fear.

"I guess I just always thought you and . . ." My sentence loses steam. How do I tell the boy I've loved since forever that I want to be a mom one day, and if he is dead set against kids, I'm not quite sure how that will work, because we're still just kids ourselves.

"I guess I could change my mind if you were my wife," he says.

"Josh," I say, my voice soft, my heart pounding. "I don't think we should talk like this. We're too young. We can't make promises we don't know how to keep."

"Would you, though," he says, "marry me if we were older?"

I smile at him. The full moon overhead. "I'd marry you, yes, if we were older, and if you wanted to be a dad one day. I mean, just imagine it, a mini Josh and Leah."

He chuckles. "I can imagine it, you know, a life with you."

My whole heart swells. Butterflies in my stomach are the least of it. "I feel like this is a dangerous conversation."

"Well, it's your birthday," he says. "Maybe it's time to have grown-up conversations every once in a while."

"You mean you don't just want to laugh about how crazy our moms are and how strict our dads are?"

Josh reaches out his hand, looking for mine, and I offer it to him. He laces our fingers together, and we hold hands like we have a hundred times, but this feels different. The words we've spoken tonight mean more.

"Tell me something I don't know about you," he says.

I swallow. "Something you don't know about me?"

"Yeah," he says. "I'm sure there's things you've kept hidden."

I shrug. "I guess some things." I pull my hand away and pump my legs to move the swing, not wanting to look at him. There's only one thing on my mind when I think about secrets that I keep.

One thing I don't dare utter.

One thing I worry would ruin everything.

"What is it?" he asks.

"It doesn't matter," I say.

"Of course it does, Leah. Everything about you matters. You matter."

"I've just seen some things," I tell him.

"What kind of things?"

I exhale, wanting this moment to be perfect and not marred by the mystery I've been following. The missing girls I can't seem to forget.

It's the kind of mystery that would unravel everything.

Our families, our futures, our church, everything.

A mystery that started when I was doing a research paper on our county, and I started reading about the missing girls, five of them, the disappearances a few years apart. All nine or ten years old.

Maybe I shouldn't have sent the email, opening the door to talk to the person I think is behind this all.

Maybe I should have just gone straight to my dad and told him what I thought.

But my dad never listens to me. He just orders me around.

And yesterday, after Dad told me I was out of line for talking back, I broke. I am tired of being made to feel small. It's how I have been made to feel all my life. What if I was strong? If I took matters into my own hands?

I went on the computer at the library and sent an email to a stranger saying I thought they were connected to the missing girls.

Now I wish I could go back in time, be less brave, not take my anger at my father out by being reckless on the internet.

But it's already done. The email was sent.

Part of me wants to tell Josh all of this, so he understands why I am so in my head, but I don't want to wrap him up in this.

"All right," he says, "let's not talk about anything unhappy then. I don't want you to be upset. It's your birthday."

I swallow, looking over at him. "So, you think your mom's really going to adopt?"

I repeat the question. It's on my mind for a reason. I'm scared for whoever this little girl might be.

"Yeah," he says, "pretty sure they're doing it. I think they're going to meet her soon. Why do you keep asking about it, anyway?"

I shrug. "I don't know. She might be my future sister-in-law."

Josh laughs, and then he stands up from the swing, walking over to me and pulling me up from mine.

"I love you, Leah."

"I love you too, Josh."

"No, not love you like you are my best friend. I love you like you are my forever." He pulls something from his pocket. "I don't have a ring, not yet, but I will one day. Until then, take this." He unfurls my fingers and places an arrowhead in the center of my palm.

"I remember this," I say.

He smiles, tucking a strand of hair behind my ear.

He bought this when we went to the Whitman Museum years ago. I remember him showing his purchase to me, how cool he thought it was. I run my finger over the smooth stone.

And then he steps closer, placing a hand on my cheek. His fingers soft. His eyes searched mine. "Can I kiss you?" he asked.

"Yes," I tell him.

And he does, and it's the kind of kiss I know, even in this moment, that I will always remember, a kiss too perfect for words, a kiss that is just ours. I close my eyes holding onto the kiss as long as I can, wanting this moment to last forever, not having the faintest idea of how quickly everything is going to end.

Never in my wildest dreams, or most terrifying fears, imagining it is the last kiss of my life.

CHAPTER 5

Annie

At the homeschool co-op, I get the kids off to their classes before finding my two closest friends, Lisa and Susannah. They're in the kitchen of Good Faith Fellowship, the church where the co-op is held. It is also the church Lisa and I have attended for our entire adult lives.

The co-op consists of a dozen families, and all but Susannah's family are members of the congregation. We've hired a few teachers to help with once-a-week extracurricular programming for our kids. At home, throughout the week, the mothers teach the other subjects — math, science, history and English. When we bring the kids here, they get to do hands-on experiments, a PE class and an art session with adults other than their moms.

The mothers use the opportunity to chit-chat in the kitchen and catch up on the week. Susannah, Lisa and I always sneak off alone, a tight-knit threesome. And honestly, with all our kids, I don't have the capacity for many more than two friends.

The other days of our weeks are full, managing our households with the kids home, so it's nice to have a chance to get some girlfriend time in on a regular basis. Over the years, this time has become so cherished.

The farmhouse is busy, and my mother-in-law is often in earshot, so I appreciate a chance to let down my guard with my girlfriends.

On the counter in the kitchen are jars of beautifully canned peaches. "Who made these?" I ask, picking one up and admiring the mason jar.

"I did," Susannah says with a smile. "I was going through my cellar and didn't want anything to expire. I thought you and Lisa could take some off my hands."

"I forgot about your cellar. You have an old house like my in-laws. Sarah's cellar is stocked like yours, and I am always so jealous." I have only been to Susannah's house a few times in all the years we've been friends. It's small, and she usually ends up joining Lisa and me at one of our homes since we have all the kids running around.

Lisa pipes up: "Canning was one hobby I never got into. I am always so impressed with it, though. The fruit of your labor is incredible," she adds, picking up one of the jars herself.

Susannah laughs. "Yeah, well, Sarah and I both only had one son each, maybe we have more time on our hands than you and your broods."

"I feel like we haven't talked in ages," I say to them both, setting down my purse and jacket on a chair at a table in the corner of the kitchen.

"How are things going?" Susannah asks. She is wearing a warm smile, and her naturally curly brown hair is loose around her shoulders. "I just heard that Josh got corralled into soccer after class today. How'd that go?"

I pour myself a cup of coffee and add creamer. "I heard it was Nathan's idea," I say, referring to her son. "I was surprised, because Nathan is usually so shy."

"Well, Nathan seems stir-crazy lately. He is at home so much with me, I am glad he wants to get out and be with friends. I was encouraging him to meet up with your boys."

"Well, he always used to love playing soccer. I don't know. He's just been so off, since—"

I watch as Lisa pulls in a sharp breath. "Since Leah?"

"Sorry," I say, "but yeah, since Leah."

Lisa's eyes immediately fill with tears. She blinks them away and reaches for a tissue in her pocket. "I'm sorry," she whispers. "I'm trying to be strong. It's just, I swear, it's so hard coming here. All I can think of is my little girl should be here too, enjoying all these moments, all these days, and instead . . ."

I reach out and give my oldest friend a big hug. "You are being so brave."

"It's all right," she says. "I have the other kids."

And she does. She has seven others. Leah was smack dab in the middle of the brood. "It's just not the same with her gone."

"I'm so sorry," I say, meaning it. "I shouldn't have mentioned Josh. It's just—"

"No, don't hold back because of me. Josh *should* be upset. *I'm upset.* He and Leah were like two peas in a pod, ever since they were little, and now . . ." She swallows. "It's all too much."

"How can I help you?" I ask her. "Let me be your support. I know I've been busy the last few months with Jubilee, and—"

"No," Lisa says, "it's not your job. Besides, John is telling me another baby could help with the loss. So maybe I will be pregnant soon."

John is her husband, and an overbearing one of that. He always tells Lisa how she should dress, how she should act, and how many more children he wants her to bear.

"I don't want to cause you any pain," I say, "I love you, and I want to be here for you however I can."

Susannah has gone quiet, which is nothing unusual. She's reserved and doesn't speak unless she has something to say, which is the exact opposite of Lisa, who always has something to fret about. Me? I'm somewhere in the middle.

"What aren't you saying?" I ask Susannah.

She shrugs. "I don't want to give advice. But maybe you should go to counseling instead of having another baby. I don't think pregnancy is going to fix Leah being gone."

Lisa frowns. "But I want to have a big family."

"You *do* have a big family," Susannah says. "You have seven beautiful children."

Lisa shakes her head. "You wouldn't understand."

Susannah goes quiet at that. She's a mom of one, which is a bit of an anomaly in this group of friends. Everyone got really into the Quiverfull movement, which advocates big families, comparing children to arrows in a quiver. It was like, who can outpace the Duggars, the reality-TV family with nineteen children to date? After five, I called it quits. Of course, with Jubilee, now there are six.

It sounds like Lisa's going to keep having children. As long as her husband John has a say in it.

But Susannah's comments cut deeper than she realizes. Maybe I should have gone to therapy instead of adopting Jubilee. I don't know who I am if I am not caring for children — I am no different than Lisa, not really.

"I know I don't have a big family like you guys," Susannah says, once her thoughts have been collected. "But I do know a thing about loss. You can't replace Leah by having another baby. It doesn't work that way."

And Susannah does understand loss, probably more than a lot of us. She lost her parents when she was young. She doesn't have extended family, and I know she wanted more children than she has, but after several miscarriages, she made peace with the size of her family. She's an example of being strong, even when life doesn't always go your way.

I'm impressed by her strength and by her ability to smile through hard things. I'm also impressed by her marriage. Her husband, Terry, is solid. I'm not saying David isn't. It's not fair to compare my marriage to hers.

But she and Terry are different than David and I have ever been. I was lost when I married David. I didn't have a family. I didn't have a support system. He entered my life and swept me off my feet, and it was a done deal in a matter of weeks. Mostly because I didn't have another choice. I needed an option immediately, or I would be living in a homeless shelter. He was my literal saving grace.

Susannah, though, was older when she got married. She and Josh met in college. She was studying cybersecurity; Josh was in med school. Their relationship was born out of shared respect and intimacy. And the fact that she isn't religious as well . . . that just changes things.

I've been in a marriage that's been dictated by the idea of submission. She has always been an equal. And even though her family is reserved — they keep to themselves and rarely reciprocate invitations — her friendship has been a constant in my life for a decade.

"Well, regardless," Susannah says, "your family size is your business, Lisa, but Annie," she says, looking over at me. "What are you going to do about Josh? If he's really struggling, then maybe he needs more than a pickup soccer game. Maybe he could use counseling."

"I don't know if David would ever agree to that," I say, taking a sip of my coffee.

Susannah shakes her head, giving me a look of pity I have never received from her before. "Maybe David doesn't get a choice."

Just then, Andrew comes into the church kitchen, his face tight with concern.

"What is it?" I ask.

"Dad just called."

"What happened?"

"It's bad," he says, looking directly at Lisa. "It's really, really bad."

27

CHAPTER 6

Leah
Six months earlier

After Josh's family leaves, I thank my parents for a special birthday celebration.

"Of course," Mom says. "You are my angel." She gives me a hug, squeezing around my shoulders.

I breathe her in, the baby-powder smell of her skin that usually lingers on an older generation, like my great grandma when I went and visited her in that convalescent home. But somehow, my mom smells the same, in the most comforting way possible. I think it's because she's spent so many years changing diapers and taking care of little ones. It's not bad, but it is distinct. I close my eyes and let her hug me more tightly.

"What is it?" I ask, when I pull away. My mom's not usually a hugger, and never so sentimental.

"You're just growing up, is all," she says. "I saw you and Josh in the backyard."

I swallow, not wanting to get in trouble. "What did you see?" I ask her. "We were just on the swing set, hanging out."

My mom nods slowly. "Well, I saw you do more than swing," she says. "I was standing at the kitchen window doing dishes, and maybe it was the light of the back porch or the moon, but he kissed you."

My body tenses, fearful that I'm going to get in trouble for something so simple, something so age-appropriate, something so sweet, my first kiss with a boy I love who's known me since I was a little girl. There couldn't be anything more wholesome than that kiss, because it was just that — sweet and pure and mine. Ours. Something to share. I don't want my mom to take it from me so quickly.

"I'm going to speak to your father about this," she says. "You know our views on physical touch with people who are not your husband."

"Husband," I repeat, my eyes widening, looking around the living room, now empty. My siblings have all gone off to bed. It's after 10 o'clock at night. I don't know where my father is, but suddenly I'm scared to see him. I don't want to be in trouble for something that felt so innocent. "Why do you have to let Dad know?"

"Because he's the head of this household, Leah. It's my job as his wife to inform him of what's going on underneath his roof."

"We weren't under his roof," I say, knowing my words are cavalier. "We were in the backyard."

"Don't be smarty with me," my mom says, tight-lipped.

"Why are you being like this?" I ask her. "It's Josh. I love him."

"Love?" Mom scoffs. "You can't know what love is when you're fifteen years old, Leah. He's going to try to seduce you and force you to do something worse."

"Seduce me? Mom, he asked if he could kiss me, and I said yes. There was nothing."

"I'm so disappointed in you."

"In me? Mom, I . . ."

"I'm going to talk to your father about this," she says. "I don't want to discuss it with you anymore. He will take your punishment into his own hands."

"Is that a threat?" I ask.

"A threat?" my mom asks. "No. Have you forgotten how you were raised? Your father is the head of this household. I'm beneath him and you are beneath me."

"I'm not beneath anybody," I say, wondering what happened to my mom. Was she always like this? So submissive, so hurtful? "I'm my own person, Mom, and I didn't do anything wrong. I kissed Josh because I love Josh, and he loves me. And . . ."

"Enough," Mom says. "I don't want you to disgrace this family. You know how we view things, how a woman's body is meant to be kept pure for her husband."

"I didn't do anything impure, Mom. I just kissed a boy. It was Josh. You love him."

Her eyes search mine. "Don't be naive," she says, and then she turns and walks away, and I'm left standing in the living room wondering what I'm doing here. What is the point of letting my own mother talk to me like that? To judge me and condemn me and make me feel small? I want to be in charge of my own life, my own destiny. And she's just hell-bent on making me pay for things I've never done wrong.

In the bathroom, I lock the door, then splash cold water on my face. When my mom gets like this, reprimanding me for simply being a teenager, I feel so frustrated. I am not doing anything reckless, anything out of line. Pressing the towel to my face, I want to scream. Why can't things feel normal for once in my life?

I pull the arrowhead from my skirt pocket, staring at Josh's symbol of love. I kiss it, not caring if it is weird, wanting to be close to him. I slip the arrowhead under my blouse, into the fabric of my bra, wanting it next to my heart.

Then, feeling rebellious in a way I have never been before, I walk to the hall closet and reach for my jacket. I zip it up to my chin, and then I walk out the front door quietly. If I'm going to get punished, I want to do something to earn the consequence.

The walk to Josh's is only two and a half miles. It won't take me long to get there, and I don't know if his mom will let me see him or what would happen when I do, but he's my closest friend and my only person, and I don't have a cell phone. I can't exactly call him and let him know I'm coming. I can't text him. I can't text anybody. I feel alone in the world, and I don't like this feeling.

It's the same feeling I had the other day when I sent that email, telling the kidnapper I was onto what they'd done.

I don't want to act foolish, but at the same time, I'm not willing to stick around and be hurt by people who are my family.

I close the front door behind me, shoving my hands in my puffer coat pockets as I began to walk down the driveway, toward the road. I turn left, headed to Josh's house, not sure what I'll do when I get there.

It doesn't really matter, though, because before I even set foot on their property, I feel hands wrap around me, a cloth pressed to my mouth.

I breathe in and I breathe out, but my eyes close, and everything goes dark.

CHAPTER 7

Annie

The church kitchen falls silent as Andrew explains to us what David had just told him on the phone.

Remains were found.

He starts crying, and I realize this is bigger than something a seventeen-year-old should share. I look at Lisa, my heart pounding, recognizing what all of this means.

Still, she hasn't clicked the pieces into place. I know it's only a matter of time before her world comes crashing down. Before the entire co-op is in tears.

My mind goes to Josh, and maybe that's wrong that it doesn't first go to Leah, but my boy is going to take this hard.

"Andrew," I say, "is Lisa's husband on his way?"

"Yes," Andrew says, "John and Dad are coming right now. I think most of the dads are."

"Okay." I nod, trying to keep myself together. "Thank you, Andrew."

"Remains?" Lisa asks. "What does that mean? Why is John coming here? I don't understand."

Susannah, though, realizes the impact of the word. She reaches for my hand as if we both need to stand as one pillar of strength to support Lisa.

"I think it means . . ." Susannah's words got lost in her throat. Tears fill both of our eyes. Before we manage to say any more, Lisa's husband is here, in the kitchen, reaching for her hands.

Susannah's husband is behind him, and he walks straight to his wife, giving her a hug. "You okay? Suzie?" He pulls her into a tight embrace. I am grateful my closest friends have supportive husbands.

David is with the other fathers, headed down the hall, looking for their children, wives and families.

Lisa's family will never be together again. Lisa's daughter is gone.

I know that to be true, even before David looks into my eyes, before he reaches out and wraps an arm around me in a warm embrace.

"What is it?" Lisa asks, her eyes searching the room. "John, tell me why you're here. What's going on? Remains of what? Remains? *Remains?*"

Then tears begin to flow as John explains the truth. "I'm so sorry. They found Leah. They found what was left of her over on Barnes Road, in the cornfield."

"What was *left* of her?" Lisa asks, bewilderment shining in her glassy eyes. "What do you mean by what was left of her? That's our little girl. She was just lost. We just have to find her. She's missing. She's been missing, but she'll be found. Won't she?"

John stays calm, and even though he's usually an over-bearing man who gets his way, in this moment, there is nothing but heartbreak in his voice. The kitchen that has held so many cups of coffee and conversation, prayer requests, and joys and sorrows as we lifted one another up over a decade as mothers and parents and teachers and friends is suddenly holding something altogether new.

It's holding the weight of a loss that none of us has ever known, not like this.

A daughter, nearly grown, gone.

John wraps his wife in his arms, and I think even though we all feared that Leah was never coming back, I don't think we really thought that her body would be found. And so close to home.

"What does it mean?" I ask David, pulling him to the side. We hear all the children moving about in the hall. The teachers have lost control of their charges, as so many parents have arrived to bring their families back together. A feeling I understand very well.

I want my children with me, too. Jubilee, especially. My little girl. I don't want her lost, either.

David looks at me, speaking softly, "They found what was left of her. Jaden told me. The forensics team was able to identify her. It's horrific, but at least there's closure."

"Closure?" I repeat. "But we still don't know who did this."

"That's true," he says, "There's a lot of unanswered questions, but trying to find the answers right now isn't going to help anything. We should get the kids. Take them home."

I nod in agreement. "I'm thinking everybody's going to be stressed out, especially Josh."

David agrees. "Let's just get the kids out of here."

I tell Susannah goodbye and I give Lisa a tight hug. "I love you. I love you so, so much."

I don't think she even hears me. She's lost in her sorrow and grief. Her daughter will never be in her arms again. Leah is gone, forever.

I go down the hallway and gather my children. When Josh sees me, though, his shoulders begin to shake. He knows.

"Is it true?" he asks, "everyone's saying that they found Leah, that she's gone, that . . ."

"Yes, Josh," I tell him. "Her body was found. She's really dead."

"No, Mom, say it isn't true." He begins to sob, falling apart in my arms, and I wrap him up against me, and he may be fifteen, nearly grown, but he's still my little boy. My little Josh.

Jubilee is tugging at my shirt. "Mama," she says, "what's happening? School's over?"

"Yes, sweetheart, it's canceled for today," I say.

"Why is Dad here?" she asks, looking behind me at David.

"We're all going home," I say. "We're going to have a nice easy day. All right?"

She frowns, her focus being on the art class she didn't want to miss. But situations change.

"Art will be here next week," I say, wanting to relieve her stress.

We can't stay here doing schoolwork, not when our community has just been shaken to its core.

* * *

Emily is back home when I arrive in the van with the kids. David is in his truck right behind us.

"You didn't want to stay with Jaden's family?" I ask.

Emily shakes her head, tears in her eyes. "No. I thought I should come home, be with Josh. It's just so awful."

I pull her in for a hug. "I know. I know it is."

"Jaden said the state police are coming in, which makes sense."

"The state police?" David asks. "Really? The local jurisdiction won't be covering the case?"

"I guess not," Emily says, having the inside scoop. Her fiancé, Jaden, is a police officer in town, so she would know.

My father-in-law, James, is on the porch with Sarah. His arm is around her shoulders, in a comforting embrace.

"I just can't believe it," Sarah says, placing a hand on her heart. "To think this is happening in our town, in our community."

"Well, it's not the first time this has happened, Sarah," James says. "There have been other girls."

"That was a long time ago," David says.

I clear my throat. "I don't mean to worry anyone, or stress anyone out, but—"

"What is it?" Sarah asks me.

"Let's go talk in the kitchen," I say, not wanting the younger children to hear. At the same time, I realize Jubilee's

35

the only *younger* child anymore. The other kids are teenagers or are grown. Still, I don't want Jubilee to know the details. As her mother, it is my job to protect her innocence.

"Mason?" I ask. "Can you take Jubilee and put on a show in the living room? Get her a snack. I don't want her to be worried. It's a lot going on."

Josh and Andrew are talking a few yards from the house, and I leave them be.

Emily, David, Sarah, James and I go to the kitchen, where we explain what we heard at the co-op. When I share about Lisa's sobs echoing the church kitchen, Sarah shakes her head, crying as she speaks. "I'm sure there will be a vigil in town."

David agrees. "I'm sure the church is already planning something. I can call Pastor Craig and find out."

"I just can't believe it," I say. "I can't believe Leah's really gone. I always prayed she would come back to us one day."

"It makes you realize how precious everything is," James says.

"Exactly, and this is what I wanted to talk to you all about," I say to my family. "Jubilee ran away when she was in foster care three or four times. It just makes me worried that she could be triggered by this news."

"She hasn't tried running away here at all," Emily says. "She loves it here."

David and I share a look. "Sure. I mean, she loves us in her own way, but you know Jubilee hasn't had a perfect transition into our family," I say gently.

James, Sarah, David, and I know the details more than our daughter Emily does. Emily has been busy working, planning her wedding, and spending time with her fiancé. She doesn't know how hard things have been.

"What do you mean?" Emily asks. "Sure, she has meltdowns, but overall, she's an angel."

Sarah clucks her tongue. "An angel who hoards food, who lies incessantly, who sneaks around the house. I've caught her in my room," she says, "looking through my things, slipping my jewelry in her pockets."

"Why didn't you tell me this?" Emily asks. "I could have watched out for her."

"No," I say, "you're our child. I don't want you to be on guard for your new little sister. I didn't think it'd be fair to either of you."

"I get that," Emily says. "But I'm an adult. Hearing more of what Juju has been going through makes me feel a little in the dark."

"Don't feel that way, I didn't want to add any more stress to your life. Your wedding is in less than three months. I wanted you to focus on yourself, on your future," I assure my daughter. "We're telling you now because it feels important for everyone to keep an eye on Jubilee. I don't know what triggered her when she ran away before, but upsetting news might be a part of it."

"You really think she would run away?" Emily asks.

"I don't know what she might do, but I'm scared. I don't want anything to happen to her. Now with Leah being taken and murdered, I just . . ."

"Murdered?" Sarah gasps. "My goodness, you think it was murder?"

"Well, what else do you think it could be?" I ask. "Why else do you think the state police are coming in? This wasn't an accident. She's been missing for months. She was found dead—"

David cuts in. "Okay. I think we all need to take a deep breath. Nothing's happening to Jubilee. She's fine. I understand why you're worried, but—"

"Do you?" I cut in. "We should have never brought her here to a town like this, where the girls were kidnapped and killed. What were we thinking?"

"Well, we didn't realize that's what happened to Leah at the time. We thought maybe she ran away. The other girls who have gone missing are all younger than her."

Josh is at the kitchen door. He's heard everything. "Leah would never have run away. She loved . . ." He swallows. "I loved her. I know that she would never . . ."

"I know you loved her," I say, wiping the tears from the corner of my eyes. Feeling a sense of fear I have never felt before.

Emily walks to Josh, giving her little brother a hug. "I'll let you guys know if I hear anything from Jaden," she tells us. "And I really hope we get some answers."

Then there's a crash in the living room.

"What are you doing, Jubilee?" Mason shouts. "Calm down! Stop crying!"

David and I lock eyes, not feeling like anything is going to be okay. Maybe ever again.

CHAPTER 8

Leah
Six months earlier

I'm completely disoriented when I awake. I am in a corner, sitting on a cold linoleum floor. The room is dim. The only light comes from a sliver underneath a door across from me.

On my hands and knees, I move to stand. A counter is beside me and I pull up. It's a sink. I look around, trying to get my bearings. I'm in a small kitchen, a kitchen that would fit in an apartment. There is a fridge, a stove and a sink.

I blink, trying to remember what happened before I got here. I was walking, still a mile or so from Josh's house. Arguing with Mom. She said I would be punished for what I had done.

A kiss, the sweetest, most perfect kiss.

My stomach rolls. I feel nauseous. The sink next to me is my saving grace as I throw up.

I hear the door crack, and I look over my shoulder, pressing my hand to my mouth.

"You're awake," the voice says.

"Where am I?" I ask.

"They just call it Home," she tells me, stepping closer.

With the door open, more light emanates into the room, and I can see her face clearly. She's a teenager, maybe a little bit older than me, with long hair. She's slender, in a nightgown that reaches the floor. I've never seen her before.

I turn on the faucet. Water runs from it as I rinse out the sink. I was raised to keep things nice and neat, never make a mess. My instincts are kicking in even now, as I clean up my vomit in a strange, unfamiliar place.

"Was I drugged?" I ask. I'm barefoot but am wearing the clothes I had on when I left my house for the walk to find Josh, minus the winter jacket. I don't remember anything.

"Probably," she says softly. "I mean, that's what happened to everyone else."

"Everyone else?" I ask. "What do you mean?"

She shrugs. "There are four of us here."

"Where?"

"Come," she says, "to the bedroom."

As I begin to follow her out of the kitchen, I notice that there is a table with six chairs in the center of the room. On the table is a change of clothes, with a note on top.

I step toward it and read:

> *Welcome home!*
> *We are so blessed to have another girl. Here is a clean dress and a nightgown for you to wear. There will be more clothes in your size shortly! Please leave your dirty clothes in the hamper. There are extra toiletries in the bathroom. If you need anything, write it on the list on the fridge.*
> *Love, Father and Mother*

I look at the girl who found me. "What is this?" I hold the note out for her to read. She steps toward me and takes it from my hand.

She shrugs. "It's how we communicate with them." She nods toward the refrigerator. I see a magnetic notepad, with a few things jotted down on it. I step toward it and read.

Colored pencils
Tampons
Nail polish remover

Past the kitchen is a small living room with a sofa, a few armchairs and a coffee table. The whole place is set up like an apartment, a nice enough one at that.

I follow her through the door into a bedroom. The room is simple, with three sets of bunk beds.

"What is this place?" I ask.

"Our room," she says, "our world."

"What do you mean, your *world*?" I ask.

She swallows. "We've been down here for a long time. Well, Tamara has been here the longest."

The other girls are crawling out from under their covers, but they're not really girls at all. They're women, young women. The youngest one looks to be about twelve or thirteen. The oldest looks like she's Emily's age.

Panic begins to rise in my chest. The eyes of the girls are hollow, and the room is musty, chilly. Like we are in a basement. The walls are cinderblocks. "Why am I here? What's happening?"

Tamara steps toward me, reaching for my hand.

"It's been a long time since we've had someone new."

My eyes widen, trying to understand, looking around to see an exit. One of the girls on the bed must understand what I'm doing, what I'm looking for.

"There's nowhere to go," she says, her voice like an echo, a warning lost in the wind. "Once you're down here, you can't get out."

"What do you mean, can't get out?" I ask, my words tight in my throat, the bile still there, making me feel sick. "What are you talking about? Who brought me here? What . . ."

"Mother and Father," she says.

"Who are your parents? You are all sisters?"

"It's not like that," Tamara tells me. "Once we were all girls from different families, and then we were theirs."

41

CHAPTER 9

Annie

I move to the sound of Jubilee's voice in the next room. Mason is trying to calm her, but she is yelling louder by the second.

"Just stop shouting," he tries to reason with her, clearly agitated.

"I want it! I want to watch that movie. I want to watch that movie now!"

"What movie?" I ask, as I walk into the living room, seeing her face streaked in tears, her fist clenched, stomping her feet.

"She wants to watch that horror movie with that creepy doll," Mason says, shaking his head.

"Jubilee." I keep my voice calm and measured. "We don't watch shows like that in our house. They're not appropriate. You're nine years old."

"I don't care. I could watch it in my old house. Maybe I should go back there," she says, her voice tight and laced with anger. "Go be with my other family, my other mom and dad."

"Hey," I say. "It's okay to express your desires and your wants."

"Is it?" she snaps.

My eyes widen. I reach for her hand, but she pulls back. Her arms cross. Mason and I make eye contact.

He shrugs and says, "I'm going to go outside to talk to Josh. He's really torn up." Mason leaves through the front door, and David joins me from the kitchen.

"Everything okay in here?" he asks.

"No," I say, pressing my fingers to the bridge of my nose. "Jubilee is mad that she can't watch that horror movie, and she says she wants to go back to her old foster home."

David crouches down in front of her. "Hey," he says. "Do you really want to take a visit to see them? Maybe we could make a plan to do that."

She looks at him with disbelief. I swallow my fear. I don't like this idea at all. I know what David's trying to do, thinking that meeting her at her level and giving her support is what's going to calm her down, but it also offers an escape. And I'm not quite interested in giving her a reward after she threw a fit.

I swallow. "We have a busy week right now. There's a lot going on. Maybe sometime soon we could talk about this, but not now," I say, stepping between David and Jubilee. I want to scream at my husband. What is he thinking?

Well, I know what he's thinking. He's thinking this is helpful, that he's jumping in and giving a good idea, but he's not. All he's doing is making matters worse.

"No," Jubilee says. "I wanna go see them now."

"Well, we can't go see them now," I say, "we have other things going on today, Jubilee. We can't always get what we want."

She scowls. "I know. I already couldn't get what I wanted today. You wouldn't let me stay home with Emily. And then you made me leave co-op."

"Everybody left co-op," I say. "And look, I see that you're upset right now because there's so much going on, but do you want to talk about that?"

"No," she says, wrapping her arms around her body, not meeting my eyes. "I don't want to talk about anything."

43

She wipes her tear-streaked cheeks and storms up to her bedroom. Her feet pound the hardwood floor with each step.

David looks at me. "What?"

"You know what," I say. "You're giving her this option, this out. We're not taking her back to her old foster family. They were not safe people."

"She could have a visit. We could meet them at a restaurant or something."

"We're not doing that," I say. "We're her family now."

"I know, but—"

"No," I say. "She just wanted to watch that creepy movie. She threw a fit about it. That is all this is. A power struggle."

David shakes his head and runs a hand over his beard. "That's not why she was upset. Annie, she's upset because of all this stuff with Leah being found. It's horrible, what's happened. She's heard too much about it. Knowing that a girl's dead body was found would freak anybody out, especially a nine-year-old."

"Okay," I say, trying to see his point of view. "Well, then we can just talk to her about that. Not make her empty promises."

"Maybe they shouldn't be empty," David says, still pushing. "Maybe seeing some people from her past would be helpful. Give her a better sense of closure."

A frown crosses my face. "I don't know, David. I don't want to trigger her with the past. I think it would just give mixed messages and be even more confusing. She's already having a hard enough time. And she's only been here a few months, not a few years."

"All right," he says. "Your call. I was just trying to make a suggestion."

"Thanks," I say. "In the meantime, can we talk about Josh?"

David exhales, showing his exhaustion. "What do you want to talk about?"

"He's not himself. He's so sad. He's depressed. This is just gonna push him over the edge. I don't know if he's going to recover. He's been crying so much, David. And that was before Leah's body was found. He needs to see a therapist."

"Of course he is upset," David says as if it's obvious, but he doesn't add that he agrees that our son needs counseling. Why is he so resistant to outside help? "Leah was his best friend," he adds. "This is devastating news."

My phone buzzes in my pocket. I pull it out and see it's a text from Susannah. "There's a vigil tonight," I tell David, reading the message to him. "At the church. I'm sure everyone will be there."

"Good," he says. "How about I stay back with Jubilee, and you go with the teenagers, if they're up for it?"

"I'm sure Josh's going to want to go," I say. "And I want to be there."

David nods. "I'll stay here with Jubilee. I don't think it's appropriate to take her tonight."

I step closer to my husband and wrap my arms around him. I let my shoulders fall as he holds me tight. "I can't believe she's dead," I whisper.

"Me either," he says, running a hand over my hair.

"She was so young," I say, "it could have been anybody. It could have been Jubilee."

"It wasn't Jubilee," he says, holding me tight. "Have faith, Annie. She's going to be okay. She's home, right where she belongs."

"We must keep Jubilee close. Leah was alone when she was taken. Nobody was watching her. Why was she out taking a walk all by herself after ten at night, anyway?" I swallow, wiping the tears from my eyes as I step away from my husband's embrace.

"We might never have those answers, Annie. We need to make peace with not knowing."

"I just hope that's the last of it," I say. "We can't have any more loss in this town. Not lost like that."

* * *

Later, I gather Emily, Andrew, Josh and Mason into the van to drive back to the church for the vigil that's been planned. Sarah, my mother-in-law, and James, my father-in-law, have already headed to the church to help with the preparations. Sarah, not working outside the house, spends a lot of her free time helping with various programs at the church, and so I'm not surprised she volunteered to help tonight.

Since I grew up without a close-knit family, they have always modeled to me what it meant to be involved. To put the time in and invest in the people you're living life with. I wonder if, back when I was looking ahead at being an empty nester and getting scared at the thought, I should have focused my energy on something besides having another child. Were my motives selfish? I push the thought away, knowing what is done is done. Now, I can be present for the choices I have made. I need to make peace with them, one way or another.

The vigil is being held at our church. On our way to Good Faith Fellowship, we pass where her body was found, my heart racing as I drive down the stretch of highway, wondering what it must have been like for her in these last moments of her life.

I'm glad there's no autopsy report yet. I don't think I'm ready to see or hear what exactly happened to her body before she died. None of us are, right now. We can go and say a prayer, sing a song, light a candle and hopefully find some peace in the middle of this tragedy.

When we park the van, we're among a few dozen other vehicles in the church parking lot. The vigil is outside, in the grassy property behind the building. I am glad to be outside, the sky growing dark, stars popping out. It allows for a stillness that being inside under fluorescent lighting wouldn't.

The kids walk away from me, looking for their friends. I do the same and see Susannah standing with her husband and son.

I walk over to them and give Susannah a hug. "How you doing?" I ask.

"It's just all so sad," she says, wiping her eyes. They're reddened, and I'm sure mine are too. "Your family doing all right?" she asks.

I press a hand to my heart. "As well as any of us could be. I'm mostly worried about Lisa. Is she here?"

Susannah shakes her head. "No, they're not coming."

"Really? This is done in support of her family," I say.

"I know, but they are emotionally spent."

I nod, feeling so much compassion for my friend. "It's all so much. They should conserve their strength for the memorial service."

We walk toward the center of the crowd. Pastor Craig from the church is handing out candles, and we light them using the wick from the person standing next to us. Soon enough, all fifty or so people who have gathered are holding a little light shining in the night sky. The choir director leads a song, Amazing Grace, and I try to hold on to the words, *how sweet the sound*, but nothing about the lyrics sound amazing or graceful. It's all just horrific; heartbreaking.

A few kids from the youth group stand up and speak, and there's a sense of it being a funeral, even though it's not. I look at Josh, wondering if he's going to go up, but he's just standing there stoically. No emotion, no tears.

"You all right?" I ask, wrapping an arm around his shoulder.

"I don't wanna be here," he says.

"Oh sweetie," I say, "she's your best friend."

"*Was* my best friend. She's gone, Mom. Someone killed her. We're standing here singing songs, lighting candles, when there's a murderer on the loose." His words send a shiver down my spine.

He's right, though. Someone did kill her. Someone who's been scot-free for months. Who could have already killed again. "Maybe Jaden will have an update. Maybe there's evidence," I say softly, wanting to be encouraging.

Josh snorts. "Yeah right. Because the police are always so good at fixing things."

"Don't be jaded," I say.

"Don't be jaded?" he repeats. "God, Mom, my best friend was murdered, and you want me to, what? Fake it till I make it?"

"I didn't say that," I say, "I just . . ."

"I get it," Josh says. "You don't want anybody to be unhappy. You think if we keep a smile on our face and say we're doing fine, it must be true."

He's angry from the top of his head to the bottom of his feet. I feel it. It worries me in a way I have never felt as a mother before. When I think about all the years raising the kids, we have never faced such a hard situation, never had to navigate this amount of pain. Even though Elijah had some tough teenage years, he came around and is doing so well now. Andrew may have an attitude problem at times — but it is all age-appropriate, all navigable with patience.

This, though, is life and death. It is evil on the loose. It is love stolen before it had a chance to grow.

It is pain I would never wish on anyone, and the fact my friend and her family are facing it, the fact my son is feeling so much of it — it breaks my heart.

After the service, I say goodbye to Susannah and wave at Sarah and James as they're getting into their car. "See you back at the house," I say, before I get in my van.

James shakes his head, talking over the top of his four-door sedan. "I worry about Jubilee," he says.

I walk closer to him. "You do? I'm surprised to hear this, because when I mentioned it in the kitchen earlier, no one seemed to take my concerns seriously. They thought I was jumping to conclusions or connecting dots that weren't there."

"Being here, thinking about what happened to Leah . . ." James shakes his head. "I don't want anything to happen to your little girl."

"I don't either," I say. "But I don't know how to protect her."

"I know," Sarah says. "We just all gotta look out for her, right?"

"Thank you," I say. "I love you both."

"We love you too," James says. "See you back of the house."

I drive the teenagers home. The van is silent. Everyone is lost in their own thoughts. Emily finally clears her throat. "Jaden texted, and they don't have any leads yet on who the killer might be," she says. "Probably shouldn't have said that."

"It's all right," I say. "Who am I going to tell, besides your father?"

When we get to the house, I relay that information to David.

He is sitting in the living room with a Sudoku puzzle book in his lap. "No suspects? Well, I shouldn't be surprised, considering the fact four girls have gone missing in this county without any leads," he says, shaking his head.

"I need a break from this; it's so heavy, David. How did Jubilee do?" I ask.

"She was mad because I told her she couldn't watch another show," he says, running a hand over his jaw, his eyes tired.

"What is she doing now?"

"She's up in her room, probably reading or drawing. But listen, I've been thinking about what you said in the kitchen."

"What about it?" I ask.

"I think you're right. We knew it was dangerous here. I mean, there have been missing person signs everywhere since Leah was abducted."

"Your dad was saying the same thing," I tell him, sitting next to him on the couch.

"Was he?" David asks, seeming surprised.

"Yeah. He thought it was probably a terrible idea, considering how dangerous this town has suddenly become."

"Do you regret it?" he asks.

"I'm scared. She should have never come here. Not when it is so dangerous out."

"I understand, Annie. But what are we gonna do now? She is already here."

Tears fill both of our eyes. Our emotions are heightened at the weight of everything that's transpired today.

Our conversation escalates, blaming one another for going through with the adoption, doubting if we are the best people to parent her.

Finally, though, we stop arguing, not really wanting to fight, just needing a release.

"Let's talk in the morning," I say.

"All right, I love you," David tells me. "And I love Jubilee, too."

I frown. "There was never a question of loving Jubilee."

"I know. I just . . ."

"It's fine," I say. "Let's just go to bed. We can try again tomorrow."

CHAPTER 10

Leah
Six months earlier

They stare at me, all four of them. They go around the room telling me their names.

Beth is twelve, with blonde hair, brown eyes, and freckles across the bridge of her nose. She's been here two years.

Carrie is twelve, too, but she's been here four. She has brown hair, dark eyes, with darker circles under them.

Lindy is seventeen. She's been here seven. She is small for her age and looks frail, like even sitting on the edge of her bed is taking effort.

And Tamara, the girl who found me in the kitchen, is nineteen, with thick, curly black hair and green eyes. She's been missing, living down here in this apartment, for ten years. Nearly half of her life.

Somehow, they are all alive.

The missing girls whom for the last few months I have read all about. Poring over interviews and photographs, as I tried to piece their case together. But none of them look like the missing person pictures I saw when researching.

Because they have all grown up, right here in this apartment.

"How did you get here?" I ask, looking at them.

Tamara reaches for my hand as we sit down on the floor. It's a thin carpet, and the other girls sit with us in a circle.

"We were all kidnapped," Lindy says. "We were eight or nine or ten when it happened, which is weird, because you seem so much older. How old are you?"

"I'm fifteen," I tell them. "It's my birthday today."

Tamara frowns. "I wonder why they took someone who is older this time?"

Beth shrugs. "Maybe they realized we're all getting bigger, all growing up, and they wanted someone our age."

"They wanted someone?" I ask. "What does that even mean?"

The girls shrug. "We don't really know," they say. "We only see her, and she mentions him, but he never comes down here."

"So, what are you saying? You've lived in this apartment for years?"

The littlest, Beth, nods. "We're going to get out one day," she says. "I just know it."

"How are you going to do that?" Carrie snaps at her. "How are you going to get out of this place? We've tried everything."

I look around the room, but even as I do it, I realize it's pointless. If these four girls have been living down here for years, they've probably scoured every square inch of this place.

"Well, how does she get in, whoever *she* is? Mother, I mean," I ask. "And what does she do when she comes?"

"There's a door in the kitchen," Tamara says.

"And you can't kill her? You can't hurt her when she comes in here?" I ask, thinking that is what I would do. Will do. The moment I get the chance.

Tamara swallows, then whispers, "We've tried, but she carries a gun with her when she comes in. She points it at us if we happen to be awake enough. If we try to fight her, there's no way we'll survive. Besides, even if we did get out of here, we would have to get past him. Most of the time she comes when we are asleep, or mostly asleep."

Carrie nods. "She puts sleeping pills in all the food because we are always so tired. Sometimes we've tried refusing to eat, but they make life worse."

I try to breathe through the fear. "Worse how?"

"By not taking out our garbage, by turning off the water so we can't use the shower or toilet, by putting on this screeching alarm that wouldn't turn off for hours."

"So they just found you and brought you here?" I ask, trying to understand why they are trapped down here.

"Well, we don't remember any of it, the kidnapping," Carrie tells me.

The kidnapping.

Four girls.

"I was at a carnival in Pritchard," Carrie continues. "That's where my family lives. Four years ago, right? It was Halloween, the week of, and I was walking around, and then I got lost, and next thing I knew, I was down here. I felt someone wrap their hands around me, but I must have been drugged. Chloroform," Tamara says. "That's what we think it's called."

"What do you mean, you think it's called?"

She shrugs. "I don't know. We all stopped going to school when we were, what, in the third grade? We're not exactly primed on science and biology and whatever else that grown-up stuff is."

"We do lots of crafts," Lindy says. "You want to see them?"

"Sure," I say.

"Can we get breakfast first?" Carrie asks. "I'm hungry."

They stand, all in their nightgowns, and it's strange being here with them. It's as if I'm a friend who's come to visit, not a girl who's just been kidnapped. When I stand, I look up, noticing something.

"In the ceiling, they're watching us?" I say, pointing to the camera.

"Yeah, there's a few in each room. That's how they knew when Lindy was trying to kill herself." Tamara says this plainly, as if a seventeen-year-old girl attempting suicide is just some basic fact of life.

"What did you try to do?" I ask her, alarmed.

Lindy shows me her wrist. "That was five years ago. We had a butter knife down here, and I sharpened it in the bathroom every day against the toilet. I thought it would be sharp enough, but it wasn't." Tears prick her eyes. "I'm sorry, sisters, for what I did."

I watch them as they offer Lindy forgiveness.

Tamara presses a hand to Lindy's back. "We're just glad you're still with us."

I walk out of the bedroom with them toward the kitchen. Tamara opens the fridge. "Oh," she says, "they must have made us a special breakfast, knowing you were going to be here."

"They?" I say, "Not just *her*?"

She shrugs. "I don't know. We just call them Mother and Father, but we never see him."

"I never knew my dad, anyway," Beth said. "My mom raised me all on her own."

They say everything simply as if I know the facts of their life, too. It's strange being down here, watching them move in this kitchen, taking out strawberries and a casserole that has premade pancakes piled in it. They place the pancakes in a microwave to warm up. Beth gets the syrup from the cupboard. Carrie reaches for plastic plates and forks.

A few minutes later, we're sitting at the table eating our strawberries and our pancakes and our syrup with glasses of orange juice. I frown. "But why?" I ask, as they're digging into the food and I'm just staring at them. "Why would anybody do this? Keep you, prisoners, in their basement?"

Tamara shrugs. "That's the thing, Leah. We stopped asking you questions a long time ago."

"How come?" I ask her.

"Because when you ask questions, you get hurt."

My jaw tenses; my stomach rolls. "I was asking a lot of questions the last few months," I tell them.

"What kind of questions?" Lindy asks.

"Questions about the four girls who went missing in this county over the last ten years. Asking questions about *you*. Reading about it. And I . . ."

"And you what?"

"I emailed the person I thought had kidnapped you, and two days later, here I am in a basement. That's not a coincidence."

"Why would you email?" Tamara asks. "Why would you reach out to someone you knew kidnapped other children?"

"I don't know," I say. "I guess I thought it would scare them into stopping."

Beth, the youngest, frowns. "Life doesn't work like that, Leah. If someone's a monster, they're not going to get nice with time. They're only going to get more mean."

CHAPTER 11

Annie

David gets ready for bed quickly, and I putter around the bedroom waiting for him to be done in the en suite bathroom. He walks out in his pajama bottoms and tee-shirt, freshly brushed teeth, walking over to me and giving me a kiss on my cheek.

"Night, love," he says. "I am actually going to work in the office for a bit, if you don't mind."

I smile at him, running my fingers through his hair, before patting his chest with my hand.

"Of course not. I'm just going to use the bathroom, and then pass out. I'm exhausted," I tell him, walking away.

I close the door to the bathroom. I lock it too, not because I am that concerned with privacy. How could I be after being married for two and a half decades? No, it's not about needing to be safe or tucked away from my husband or my family. I'm just wanting a moment to myself, to think. All day long, I've been going, running on all cylinders.

First it was getting the kids to co-op, hearing about Leah's death, and then the vigil. The fact that Leah is dead, truly gone, weighs heavy. All my children are going to be needing emotional support in the coming weeks as they grieve the loss of a dear friend, and as their mother, I know that will rest on me.

It's hard for me to fathom that she's really gone, that someone took her life, and that it was so close to my home. It makes me wonder who did this and how they got away with it, especially considering she wasn't the first of her kind, the first girl to go missing, never to be found again.

I swallow as I turn on the hot water at the sink to wash my face, knowing that's not quite right, because Leah *was* found. Her body has been found, and recovered. I reach for my facial cleanser and pump some into my hand, lathering my face, my eyes closed as I try to rid myself of the horrible images running like a movie through my mind.

Leah's body in the cornfield, bones broken, eyes hollow, a beautiful young girl gone.

I splash water on my face, turning off the faucet and reaching for a hand towel, pressing it against my cheeks. My whole body shivers at the thought of something happening to one of my children, one of my girls.

I don't worry about Emily. She's nineteen years old, engaged to a police officer. I feel like she's going to be safe no matter what happens.

It's Jubilee I worry about. She's so young and vulnerable, and doesn't know this place or the people here. What if someone came for her next? What if I brought her home only for her to be taken?

I need to stop that line of thinking. It's not going to get me anywhere, and it's just living in fear. I don't want to be that kind of person, gripped with catastrophic thinking, but still, as I rub moisturizer on my face and then run a comb through my hair, I can't help but feel a pang of nausea. I don't want anything to happen to my children.

My pajamas are on a hook on the bathroom door, and I change quickly, putting my clothes from the day in the hamper and then pulling on the nightgown. It hangs to my knees, floral, sleeveless, simple. David seems to like it, but I'm not interested in being intimate tonight. Tonight, I just want to close my eyes and go to sleep. I want morning to come faster than it's ever come before, because I hope against hope that a new day, a new dawn, will bring a sense of calm, of peace.

But I'm old enough to know nothing is quite that simple. And oftentimes, the things we wish for the most are the very things we never get.

* * *

In the morning, I'm in the kitchen making pancakes, my eyes darting over to the clock. It's 7:20.

By 7:30, I always wake everyone up if they haven't already puttered out their bedrooms looking for food. With three teenage boys in the house, it's rare that the smell of bacon and pancakes won't get them out of bed. Today is no exception. Andrew, Josh and Mason are in the kitchen reaching for plates, forks and maple syrup at 7:30 exactly.

"Does anybody want blueberries in theirs?" I ask.

The boys shake their heads. Josh reaches for a tub of peanut butter from the pantry, wanting to spread a layer of that on his flapjacks. And I smile, figuring the extra protein is good for a growing boy.

"Do you mind if I meet Nathan later at the indoor soccer club? His dad is coming, too."

I smile, relieved that he wants to spend time with Nathan, Susannah's son. And happy to hear Nathan's dad, Terry, is joining them. Terry is a wonderful dad, and having positive adult influences in my kids' life is of high value to me. "Of course. I don't think we have anything on the family calendar today."

"Hey, where's Juju?" Andrew asks. I frown, surprised she isn't already at the table.

"Don't think she's gotten up yet," Josh says.

"I'll go get her," Mason says, pushing away from the table.

I watch as he goes. "Thank you."

He waves a hand over his head as if it's no big deal, and I suppose it's not. It's just a brother doing his part. But a few moments later, he returns.

"Mom," he says.

"Yeah, honey?" I turn from the stovetop as David enters the kitchen dressed in his Carhartts and a clean tee-shirt, with a scruffy jawline and bright eyes. He must have slept well last night, and for that, I'm glad.

"What is it?" David asks Mason.

"Well, Jubilee's not here," Mason says.

"What do you mean?" I ask, flipping a pancake.

"I mean, she's not in her room. It's empty."

"Oh, I'm sure she's in the bathroom," David says. "Jubilee," he calls out. "Breakfast time."

But there's no answer.

"Where's Emily?" Josh asks.

Andrew jumps in. "I saw her about half an hour ago, leaving for a run."

I smile. "She's prepping for that marathon in Seattle in the fall. She has a fourteen-mile run this morning."

"I'm impressed," Andrew says. "When Emily goes for something, she goes all in."

I like my son's assessment of his older sister. "That's the kind of girl you should be looking for," I tell him.

He rolls his eyes, not wanting to hear any dating advice from his mom. When Jubilee doesn't exit the bathroom, I look over at David.

"Where do you think she'd go? Outside in the orchard?"

"I'll go find out," David says.

"All right," I say. "Let me know if you need me to help look."

He begins calling for her. I can hear him from where I stand at the kitchen sink.

"Jubilee? It's Dad. Jubilee!"

Josh pushes out from the chair at the table. "I can finish eating later. I'm going to go help Dad find Ju."

"All right," I say. "I mean, I appreciate it."

"I'm going to go, too," Mason says.

I smile, appreciating my son's initiative.

David steps inside the kitchen, shaking his head. "Can't find her."

"Do you think something could have happened to her?" I ask. Suddenly my deepest worry feels possible. No. What happened to Leah cannot happen to my girl, too.

"Can someone go check the bedroom again?" I ask, trying to remain calm, but I feel the panic rising, my worst fear surfacing. "Or maybe she's hiding in a closet or something, playing a game."

David looks at me like I've lost the plot.

"What?" I ask, annoyed at the look he gives me. "She's a little girl. Maybe she's playing hide-and-go-seek. Jubilee," I call out. "Jubilee, are you hiding?"

But after five minutes of looking around the house in every closet and behind every door, the boys and I realize Jubilee's not here.

"Maybe she went to your dad's," I say to David.

He shrugs. "Okay, I'll go over and ask, but she doesn't usually do that. It's still early in the day."

I nod in agreement, but still, he takes his cup of coffee off the kitchen counter and heads out the back door. I watch through the window that's over the kitchen sink as he walks over to his parents' house just behind ours.

His mom walks outside, and I see David talking with her. She shakes her head, and then she walks right back with him over to our place.

"Where is she?" she asks.

"I don't know, Sarah," I tell her, feeling a tightness in my chest. "That's what I'm hoping to find out."

Last night, this was what I was worried about, that something would happen to her, that she would go missing, that bringing her here was a mistake.

"It doesn't make any sense for her to leave early in the morning without saying anything," Sarah says. "Unless something happened last night. Was there a fight?"

I shake my head. "No. Not at all. I mean . . ."

I look over at David, remembering our stressful conversation about our newest daughter when I got back from the vigil. But it wasn't about Jubilee. It was about us and our choices, and how we can be the best parents possible for her. And she was in bed when we spoke . . . unless she somehow heard us. If she was out of bed and listening . . .

I think of the words we said: *We shouldn't have brought her here; it was a mistake* . . .

"Maybe we should call the police," I say.

David runs a hand over his jaw. "Really? Maybe she's just out in the woods."

"Well, go look for her there, then," I say.

And so, we all do. Everyone begins to look around the property, in the backseats of the cars, in the tractor, in the barn that David and his dad use to store all their tools and lumber for their jobs, in the garden behind Sarah and James's house.

Forty minutes later, we rally in our front yard.

"Where could she have gone?" I ask breathlessly.

Josh tenses. "We looked everywhere, Mom. I don't think she's here."

"You think she's . . ." I shake my head, not wanting to admit he is right.

"I think she might be gone," Andrew said.

"This can't be happening," I say. "She can't be gone. She's just a little girl, our little girl. She was here in her bed last night. I remember. I . . ."

I stopped then, wondering why didn't I go to her room last night after my conversation with David? Why didn't I walk into her room and open the door and make sure she was asleep? Well, I know why. The idea of waking her seemed selfish, so I kept her door closed as I passed it in the hallway.

Now, though, I try to remember what she looked like the last time I saw her. Before the vigil she threw a fit, upset she couldn't come with me, saying I must not love her if I wouldn't let her come along. I sat with her in my lap, promising her that I loved her and that her dad would tuck her into bed. I left the house knowing she was distraught and feeling like nothing I said would soothe her.

Now she is gone.

David's on the phone. I was so lost in my thoughts I didn't even register he was placing a call.

"He's talking to Jaden," Sarah says, filling me in.

My father-in-law, James, stands with us. He'd been looking around the property, too, and he rests a hand on Sarah's shoulder, worry in his eyes.

"Jaden will know something," he says. "Or he'll know what to do next."

A few minutes later, David gets off the call and walks over to us.

"What'd they say?" James says.

"They're going to put out an Amber alert, then they'll come out here and search the property."

"In that order?" Sarah asks.

David shakes his head. "No, no. I guess they're going to come here first and they're going to look around. If they can't find anything, they're going to put out the alert then, and . . . I don't know, I feel . . ."

"Are you all right?" I ask, looking at my husband. He seems flustered in a way he never is. There are beads of sweat on his brow.

Our sons stand with us, and Emily is running back onto the property as we speak. She must have been out on a run for ninety minutes. She's dripping in sweat and has missed everything.

"What's going on?" she asks, catching her breath, her hands on her knees. She looks between us. "Why is everyone here?"

"We can't find Jubilee," Mason says, straight to the point.

"What do you mean, can't find her?"

"Just that," I say. "We've been looking all over and she's nowhere to be found. I think our little girl is lost."

CHAPTER 12

Leah
Five months earlier

Nothing about the apartment feels comforting. Four weeks, I've been down here. Time is moving at a snail's pace. How have the girls survived this for so long?

Is this going to be my life forever? It's been Tamara's for *ten years*. Every time I think about that, I feel sick.

I hardly ever keep anything down, which I know is upsetting "Mother," whoever the hell she is.

Hell. That's not a word I ever used growing up. It was forbidden. And even now, it feels foreign on my lips, but I know what the Bible meant when it talked about a place you would go and feel like you were literally on fire.

I am in hell being here. I feel like I'm dying from the inside out. And everything that I used to rely on to get me through the day no longer works.

I can pray for hours, but it's not changing the fact that I'm locked up down here. I can sing songs to myself, the hymns we used to sing at church. None of them give me the solace they used to. I can spend time with my new sisters, making crafts and cleaning the place, which are things I used to do at my house, that would give me so much joy.

I would help Mom with the chores until the house was spotless and shining, and I used to find so much pride in it. But now, I feel pride in nothing, excitement in nothing, joy in nothing, because I am trapped in a box. And there's no way out.

We've gone over it, the girls and I, over and over, every day, until Lindy shouted at us, "This is stupid!" She said that they were listening, that unless we were talking underneath our covers, it was pointless to make a plan, because they would know about it.

She's right. Of course, hatching a scheme when we were being monitored was ridiculous. That wasn't going to be the way we would get free. But what was? Today is like every other day of the month. The last thirty days have been on repeat.

There's always breakfast in the fridge when we wake, which tells me the girls are right. We really are getting drugged. Whatever medicine or sleep aid they're putting in our food is strong. We have no pots or pans in the kitchen, no groceries to use to cook. We get everything pre-made and delivered in the fridge.

At first, I did what the girls warned against. I refused to eat for the first five days I was here. By the end, I was so hungry. And the girls were so angry with me, and rightly so.

No one could take a shower for days, and the toilet wouldn't flush. The whole apartment smelled disgusting, and it was my fault. I knew that. Was I going to let them suffer, because I was putting up a fight and not eating? Because the thing is, all that I accomplished was being hungry, constantly upsetting everyone else I lived with, and getting no closer to an escape.

Sure, I was alert and could potentially see "Mother" when she came in to bring food. But I still never saw her.

She knew I wasn't eating from what she saw on the cameras, so she came prepared.

Whenever she came in, I couldn't get out to see her, because they locked the metal bedroom door remotely. I would jostle the doorknob, I would kick the heavy door, and there would be no response from the other side.

I heard her, though, heard her footsteps, heard her moving in the apartment. She would take our dirty clothes in a hamper, and a few days later, they'd return, folded in a basket, waiting for us in the kitchen when we got up in the morning.

There was a system here, an order, an absolute plan, and I had learned, after a month, that me putting up a fight by not eating or showering or using the bathroom wasn't going to hurt anybody but me.

There is only one thing that is mine and mine alone.

The arrowhead.

When I changed that first morning, out of my clothes and into the dress "Mother" left out for me, I realized it was still hidden in my bra. I didn't pull it out, not wanting it on the camera, and knowing I needed to keep it hidden if I wanted to keep it.

Sometimes I know Mother and maybe even Father come in the bedroom when we are passed out, because it will be clear our hair was brushed or our nightstands tidier than they were when we lied down.

Today, in the kitchen, we're getting plates out for lunch. "This is a good meal," Carrie says. "We never get macaroni and cheese like this."

"Homemade, too," Beth says, with a smile.

How can they smile, though? I wonder, looking at them. We're prisoners, and there's no escape.

"Ooh," Lindy says, her eyes bright. "Chocolate chip cookies, too."

I roll my eyes. "Great, and after we have this delicious meal, we'll fall into a coma for three hours."

That's what usually happens after we eat lunch. We take a long nap in the afternoon, a forced nap, like we're babies, like we're toddlers, like we're incapable of surviving without an afternoon rest. In reality, they want us to be comatose, so we do what they want.

"It's not going to help, you know? Making a fuss about everything," Tamara says.

"I didn't say it was," I say, rolling my eyes. "But it's pretty messed up. Don't you think?"

"It's all messed up, but that doesn't change anything. What are you going to do? Not eat lunch? Not have a cookie? Put us all through torture, because of your choice? Of course not," she says.

"Well, I don't like this," I say.

"None of us like this, but this is our life. Make the most of it. Isn't that what Anne Frank did?"

"You're seriously comparing our situation to World War Two?" I scoff.

"No," she says. "But she didn't have a choice about where she was, and yet, she still found joy. She still found hope."

"You have hope right now?" I ask Tamara. "You've been here for half of your life in this apartment. Your skin is so pale, and it's nearly translucent. Something's wrong with Lindy. She's more lethargic than the rest of us. She needs a doctor. I think she's actually sick, anemic or something worse."

But the girls stop what they're doing and walk over to me, where I am setting glasses of water on the table.

"We've been talking," Carrie says.

"What have you been talking about?" I ask.

"About you, about your behavior, how it's not working for us. Before you came, there was all peace, all harmony, all love, and you're making it difficult," Tamara says. "We want to get along. We need you to help us."

"Help you get free?" I say.

Lindy sighs. "No. We need you to help us create peace in our lives again. There's too much discord."

"Fine," I say, pressing my fingers to my temples. "I'll do what you want. I'm not trying to make your lives difficult," I say, looking in their eyes. "I'm just trying . . ."

"We know," Tamara says. "But how you're going about it isn't working. We need to come at this with a different angle, because we're not going to be able to claw out the cinder block walls, and we're not going to be able to take down a woman who comes in here at night with a gun."

I nod, realizing she is right.

We have to think differently. We have to do differently. And unless we do that, we'll never be set free.

CHAPTER 13

Annie

By mid-afternoon, the situation has grown increasingly grim. The police have been here for hours looking for Jubilee. They said that usually it takes twenty-four hours before a missing person case is filed and a search begins, but it's different when it comes to children.

And since no one has seen her since 9 p.m. last night when she went to her room, we're nearing that mark ever so quickly.

My closest friends are here to support me. Terry, Susannah's husband, came with their son Nathan, and Lisa's husband, John, is here with their brood of children as well. Everyone is here to help search for Jubilee. We are in the kitchen with coffee, cleaning up from the lunch rush that just finished. We'd made sandwiches for everyone out looking. I am so grateful for friends who show up to help, especially when I know they have so much going on in their own lives. Lisa especially.

"You shouldn't have come," I say to Lisa. "Not with everything you're going through right now."

But she shakes her head. "Leah's been gone for six months. We've been preparing ourselves for this, and even though now it's real, it's almost like I'm numb to the grief, the reality."

She wraps her fingers around the coffee cup in her hand, sitting at my kitchen table staring out the window. Children are outside playing with hula hoops and jump rope, and the scene is a little jarring, if I'm being honest. Younger children laughing, unaware of the situation, when so much is happening in my heart. Jubilee is gone, and I don't know what to do to find her.

"Still," Susannah says to Lisa. "You need to be planning a service. The memorial. Can I help with that?"

Lisa exhales slowly. "It's really all covered," she says. "The pastor and my sister are coordinating things. As I said, this isn't really a surprise to anybody. We knew Leah was gone. We just didn't know who took her, and we still don't. Until I know that part, that piece, I don't think I'll truly have rest."

Susannah's gaze meets mine, and I wonder if she's thinking what I'm thinking.

"What?" I ask, my chest feeling tight, my eyes feeling raw and red.

"I was just wondering how you're doing," she says to me, softly. "You wanted Jubilee to come home so badly, you convinced David to agree to the adoption, and now . . ."

If she were to reach out and touch me right now, I think I would flinch because I feel so unsettled, so scared.

"You think those things aren't running through my mind, too?" I squeeze my eyes shut. "I think I have been selfish."

"What about?" Lisa asks.

"Why was I so intent on adopting Jubilee in the first place? I think I've been using motherhood to avoid facing the fact that I've never figured out who I wanted to be apart from them. I feared the kids getting older, so I had more kids."

"Like me?" Lisa asks.

I swallow, looking over at Susannah, feeling guilty for having any of these thoughts.

"I know that is what you must think, but it is more than that," Lisa explains. "It is also about God's will. Children are a blessing from heaven."

I press my lips together. Susannah fills the silence, "Take God out of it — you can't use children as a way to avoid becoming your own person."

"What are you going to do when Nathan graduates and moves to college?" Lisa asks Susannah.

"I've thought a lot about it. I don't need to work. Terry's practice supports us, but I am hoping he will retire early. Maybe we can travel the world."

Susannah's husband is a family practitioner and I know they do well for themselves. "Where do you want to go?"

"Anywhere. Everywhere. But listen, not having more children was never my plan. I wanted a bigger family too, not because it was God's will, but because I wanted more kids. I would have loved to have a daughter. But sometimes life doesn't go as planned."

"You don't have to tell me that, Susannah," I say, my voice tighter than I mean for it to be. "Jubilee is gone and police are scouring the city for her."

"Do you think it's a coincidence that Leah goes missing and her body's found, and then that very same night, Jubilee's gone?" Lisa asks. "Do you think the same person could have taken . . ."

But Susannah shakes her head. "Stop it," she said. "We have no reason to think they're connected, and besides, we still don't know that Leah was taken. She could have run away. She could have been on her way back home when she was found in the cornfield."

"No. Someone killed her," I say. "Sorry," I add, looking at Lisa.

Her eyes fill with tears and she just shakes her head. "It's the truth, Susannah. Even if Leah wasn't abducted, someone killed her."

"Still," Susannah says calmly. "At this point, there's no reason to start thinking of the worst-case scenario. We have no reason to think that these two situations are connected. Leah was fifteen years old. Jubilee is nine."

"What does that have to do with anything?" I ask.

Susannah shrugs.

"I don't know. I'm trying to make a profile of a person who would kidnap children or teenagers. Look, I don't know. I just don't want you assuming the worst."

"At this point, though," Lisa says, with a sigh that's so heavy, the whole room seems to collapse, "it *is* the worst case. My daughter is dead and Jubilee is gone."

Right then, Jaden enters my kitchen. He's in his uniform, and even though he's twenty-three years old, he looks so mature. Every time I see him, I feel a sense of confidence. Emily is only nineteen years old, so young to be settling down and getting married, but at the same time, I know Jaden is a solid man who will provide for her. And when I look at him, he's not just a young adult. He looks so grown, so capable.

"Annie," he says.

"Please tell me there's some good news," I say. "Is there an update? Is there?"

"Say something positive," Susannah says, cutting me off. "Jaden, Annie's sure that these two situations are connected, Leah and Jubilee, and I can't convince her otherwise."

Jaden reaches for a coffee mug and pours himself a cup. He takes a drink, then reaches for the sugar bowl, adding two scoops to his coffee. "Look, Annie. The thing is, we've gone through her room and her things, and Emily noticed something that made us think Jubilee might not have been kidnapped."

"What do you mean?" I ask. "I've been through her room, and . . ."

"I know you have," he says. "But Emily is the one who noticed that her backpack was missing."

I frown. "Her blue backpack?"

"Yes," he says. "There's no backpack in her room whatsoever, and the window was left open. Of course, there's nothing we can do to confirm this, but if someone snuck into her room and kidnapped her, she certainly wouldn't have had time to grab a bag."

"So you think she ran away?" I am trying to piece together this information in my mind, knowing she has a history of running away when stressed. At least, that is what the reports from CPS described.

We read through them all before we brought her home. And while she has had emotional struggles the last few months, she has never been a flight risk. I'd hoped that would always be the case.

"Okay, if she ran away, then she'll come back home," I say, processing aloud. "She couldn't have gone that far. She's a child."

Jaden nods. "Exactly. There's no reason to assume the worst."

Susannah reaches out for my hand and squeezes it. "See? Those were the exact words I was just saying."

David enters the kitchen from the back door. "What's the update?" he asks.

Jaden tells him about the backpack. "Detective Montgomery is assigned to the case — he's on his way here now, to speak with you both."

"I'm going to go and look in her room," I say, pushing away from the table. "I'm going to make sure the bag isn't there."

Jaden nods, letting me pass, and I walk into my daughter's bedroom, trying to see this through her eyes.

Why would she want to run away? Why would my little girl not want to be here? She'd only been home for a few months. She was happy. I know she was. She loves the house and her grandparents and the co-op and church and me.

She loves us, doesn't she?

I look at the hook at the back of her door, where the bag usually hangs. It's not there, and it's not in her closet, and it's not under her bed, and it's not behind her dresser. It's gone. And Jaden is right. She took it, and even though it makes me feel slightly better, the idea that she took a backpack filled with her favorite things and snuck through the window in the dead of night is still a heartbreaking reality.

My little girl wasn't taken. My little girl ran.

CHAPTER 14

Jubilee
Three months earlier

Annie isn't like anyone I've ever known before.

I mean, I remember my birth mom, and I knew my foster moms, of course, but none of them seemed to care about me that much. It was like I was in the way, like a bother, like me being with them was something they had to live with instead of what they wanted to live for.

I thought that's just how moms were. Then I met Annie. And Annie is different than anyone I've ever known.

In the mornings, she's always in the kitchen cooking something or cutting up fruit or pouring glasses of orange juice. I know it's a simple thing. I know some kids might not even know it was a big deal, but it is. Her kids don't seem to think so.

I mean, they're nice to her, but they don't seem to get how different she is. They say thank you or whatever, but they don't know how special it is to have a mom who scrambles eggs and then puts them on your plate and then asks if you want ketchup with your hash browns, and gets the bottle out of the fridge for you. Then takes your plate away and brings it to the sink when you've finished eating, and does it all over again for the next meal. Only that meal might be peanut-butter-and-jelly sandwiches cut up into little squares, with potato chips and fruit salad and iced tea that she made from the sunshine out on the back porch, that she let brew all afternoon.

She says things like, "I don't think kids are supposed to have caffeine, but my grandma taught me how to make sweet tea, so I'm making this for you." Then she drops in a slice of lemon, a real lemon, like that she's cut up on the kitchen counter.

Mason and Josh and Andrew and Emily, they seem to think it's just normal, that that's just what you get when you come to the kitchen. A plate of food, always ready. A mom standing there smiling, caring.

It's a lot sometimes. It's a lot to sit at that table with all of these kids, all of them smiling.

I know they're not all perfectly happy. Annie will say Andrew is being a grump or give Josh hugs, telling him it's all going to be okay. His best friend's been gone for a while, and it makes him cry sometimes.

When we eat dinner, we hold hands, and we pray. David bows his head and he says a prayer for all of us. I don't really know a lot about praying, but I do know this: when he closes his eyes, it's like he's making a birthday wish, but better. He says things like, "Bless Jubilee, keep her safe and healthy, and help her know that she is loved." He actually says those things.

I guess what I'm saying when I'm saying all this is that, before I came here, I thought I understood what a mom was and what a dad was. I thought I understood what family meant, because I'd see it in TV shows or movies. But it turns out I was wrong about all of that, because family is more than all that. And this family is showing me what love is.

The funny thing is, it doesn't have to do with big birthday presents or gifts under a Christmas tree. There's no *stuff* about it at all.

You know it's love, because it's slices of apples with a scoop of peanut butter because Annie thinks I just might want an afternoon snack. It's a second snickerdoodle cookie when they're fresh from the oven, with a glass of milk, while I sit on a stool at the kitchen counter, Annie laughing, saying, "I always wanted a daughter with a sweet tooth just like mine."

That's when my heart gets filled with happiness, full of love. Love. Love.

A love I never knew before.

Now that I have it, I don't ever want to let it go.

CHAPTER 15

Annie

Jaden's parents, Shanice and Marcus, drop off several casseroles for the crew that has been out looking for Jubilee
all day. I unpack them in the kitchen with Susannah. Lisa's
outside with her children and husband. I don't know why
they're still here. I say as much to Susannah as we pull back
foil from a lasagna.

"I think she's here because going home," Susannah
says, "is heartbreaking. Can you imagine going back to your
house after finding out your daughter's dead, after you've
been holding on to some shred of hope for six months? No.
This is a good distraction. It's keeping them all occupied."

"Do you think she's really going to have another baby?"
I ask, remembering the conversation yesterday morning
at the co-op kitchen, how Lisa had said that her husband
wanted another child.

"I don't know. But I'm betting yes. I mean, after the
conversation earlier today, too, it seems like she will do anything to be happy," Susannah says, with a shrug.

"Would you do anything to be happy?" I ask her, thinking about my desire to stay in perpetual mommy-mode.

Her eyes meet mine, her words even and true. "I think so. I love Terry and Nathan and want a long happy life with them . . . and if something happened to either of them, I think I would feel lost. I might do something drastic." She sighs. "But that isn't what Lisa is doing. Even before Leah went missing, she let John walk all over her."

I bite my bottom lip. "She trusts that he's the head of her household."

Susannah's eyebrows raise. "What do you think about all that?"

"You know what I think," I say. "I have faith. But David and I are equals."

Susannah presses her lips together. "Are you?"

I frown. "What do you mean? Of course."

"I don't know," she says, with a bit of a laugh. "I actually think you're the one wearing the pants in this relationship."

"Oh, really?" I say. "How so?"

"Well, you're the one who wanted Jubilee," Susannah says. "You were the one who was pushing for that, and David went along. Not every man would do such a thing. It was a big decision, and David trusted you to make it. I don't think Lisa would have as much luck with her husband."

I nod, pulling up in a drawer and reaching for a pile of forks before setting them on the counter. "Would Terry trust you to make big decisions like that?"

She smirks. "I definitely wear the pants, too."

I bite my bottom lip. "I get what you mean, though. David trusts me and I trust him. We have a good marriage."

"I'm glad," Susannah says, "because you've been married a long time."

"So have you," I say.

"Yeah," she says. "I have. But you guys have been through a lot more than I've been through. My life has always been quiet, comparatively. I mean, you have all the kids and your in-laws live right here. It's a lot, Annie."

I shrug. "I don't have much family on my side. My parents never spoke after they divorced; they went separate ways.

I never had a soft place to land. Then my mom died when I was in high school. Last I heard, my dad was drunk on a beach in Florida. After he didn't return my phone calls for half a decade, I stopped trying. It's why I always felt like I won the lottery when I met David and was welcomed into his life. It was like a whole world I wasn't expecting, and it was offered to me so freely. It was full of love, and welcoming arms. The moment I met David, I knew what family was for the first time." I pause. "We offered that life to Jubilee, you know? And if she ran away, if she didn't want it . . ." I shake my head.

"Don't," Susannah says. "She's just a child. Whatever was going through her mind before she climbed out that window wasn't logical. She was spun up with emotions. Maybe she'd heard you and David talking. Maybe she . . ."

I cut her off. "Maybe she didn't think she was wanted?"

"Even if she did think that," Susannah says, soothing me, "it's not the truth. You know that. You're a grownup. She's a child. They don't see things as nuanced as we do."

Lisa joins us in the kitchen.

"What are you guys talking about?" she asks.

Her younger children have followed her in, and hold on to her leg.

"I think I need to get these kids home," she says. "It's been a long day. But tell me, what was I missing?"

Susannah shrugs. "We were just talking about Jubilee and how kids sometimes don't have a full picture of what's really going on in a family. Maybe she made a choice in the moment to run away that she wouldn't have made otherwise."

Lisa's children run off through the living room and out the front door. She turns to us.

"Jubilee's going to come home. They're going to find her. It's only been a few hours, and she couldn't have gotten far. She's probably in the woods somewhere, thinking she's camping out."

"I like your optimism," I say.

Lisa walks over to me and gives me a hug as she says goodbye. She pauses in the embrace. "I do wonder, though, once Jubilee comes home, are you sure you want to go through with the adoption?"

I pull back from the hug, shocked at the words. "What do you mean? Send her back? She's my child, my daughter." I shake my head, confused.

"But it's not finalized yet, right? Not for a few more months, and I just wonder, if this is all the trauma and heartache she's causing now, what's it going to be like down the line?"

Susannah steps in. "Lisa, that's not appropriate, and it's totally uncalled for. I would do anything to have a daughter like Jubilee. She is a sweetheart."

Lisa is flustered and shaking her head, using her hands to speak. "I wasn't meaning anything. I was just . . ."

"It's all right," I say. "You're looking out for me, and I appreciate that. But Jubilee's not going anywhere," I say. "Once she gets home, she's staying put."

Lisa leaves, realizing she's upset me. I look at Susannah, a silent conversation exchanged. How dare Lisa say that? Who says a thing like that? Does Lisa truly think we would send our child away?

David comes in, exhaustion written on his familiar face.

"Oh, good timing," I say. "Dinner's ready. Brooke's parents brought it over."

"Oh, honey." David walks over towards me, pulling me into his arms. The hug is nothing like Lisa's. This one is tight, fierce and fearful.

"What?" I ask. "What is it? Say something." I pull away, pressing my hands to his chest, looking in his eyes, searching them for some sort of meaning, some sort of truth. "What aren't you saying?"

"We found her backpack," he says, in a hushed voice. "Well, the cops did."

I frown. "What do you mean?"

"It was on the edge of the property line in the back forty, near the tree house."

"Was she in the tree house?"

He shakes his head. "She wasn't, and . . ."

"And what?" I say, tears spilling down my cheeks. "She wasn't in the tree house. So where was she?"

"We don't know," he says. "But her backpack was found on the edge of the property."

"What does that mean? What aren't you saying?"

"I'm saying," David says, "we think she was taken."

CHAPTER 16

Leah
Four months earlier

I've never seen her face.

In the two months I've been trapped down here, I haven't seen the woman who wanted me as her new daughter. The woman who locked me up in a dollhouse of her own making is still a ghost to me.

"Is it unusual for me not to see her in all this time?" I ask at dinner. The five of us girls are sitting around the kitchen table eating spaghetti and meatballs with glasses of milk and salads dressed in ranch. It's so normal, the food, the lighting, the furniture, but nothing about it makes sense. It's twisted and sick and bizarre. "How many times have you seen her face?" I ask them.

They shrug. "It's been a while. She must only come in when we're sleeping," Lindy says.

"I wish the medication wasn't so strong," I say. "I want to see who she is. I want to look in her eyes. I want to make her pay." My eyes flick up to the camera, regretting my words instantly.

Even after two months, I still forget that I'm being watched. And we don't know if they can hear us, but our guess is that they can. They must have some sound system hooked up, because when I say things like that, when I get fired up and snippy, we all pay for it.

In the morning when we get up, we will discover a note on the kitchen table in the morning saying:

> *There will be no dessert today because of your outbursts at dinner* or *No hot water today because you were being negative about our family members.*

It's passive-aggressive at best. In reality, it's physical and emotional abuse.

If I were down here alone, I would have more resistance, but I am living with four other girls. I fear they will do something to me if I completely disregard their wishes. It is a complicated ecosystem.

I press my fingers to my eyelids, rubbing out the constant dull headache that's persisted since I moved down here.

I miss the sunlight and the blue sky and the grass. I miss Josh. I miss my mom and dad, my brothers and sisters. I miss everything. I miss co-op. I miss church. I miss laughing with my friends. I miss getting a hug from someone who's known me since forever.

I pick up my fork, shoveling the spaghetti into my mouth. I must say the food is delicious, but that doesn't make up for the fact that I'm a prisoner. "I just don't get it," I say. "It's so sick and twisted."

"Stop," Carrie says, kicking me under the table. "It's not helping things."

"What would help?"

She frowns. "I don't know. I just want a violin."

"You don't even know how to play," Beth says.

"I can learn. I want to learn!" Carrie says emphatically, looking up at the camera. "I would love a violin. I want to play an instrument. I miss music. I remember my big sister playing music." Her words get softer. Her shoulders fall. She's twelve years old and has been here since she was eight.

What is it like to grow up without a mother who loves you? It's too painful to consider.

I swallow. "Look, I want you to have your violin, Carrie, and I want all of us to get dessert and hot water and everything else. I just . . . I'm having a hard time being down here. I don't know how you've all done it so long."

"Can we talk about something else?" Tamara says softly. She's the one who seems most content with the situation, and I'm guessing it's because she's been down here for a decade. This is what she knows, all she remembers.

"Maybe after dinner and getting ready for bed, we can braid each other's hair," she says. "We got that new book on how to do fancy ones." She looks over at the coffee table in the sitting area.

Like I said, we're completely set up like a little house. It's homey, even, because the girls have put a lot of time into decorating with the blankets they've knit and the doilies they've crocheted.

Most mornings, there's some new trinket for us to enjoy. A basket of yarn or scraps of fabric, needles and threads, a coloring book or puzzle or math workbook. And these little rewards are enough to keep the girls in line, but that's because they've forgotten what it's like to be outside. They're dulled to the magic of real life.

They've been conditioned to think this is enough, but it's not.

Still, I watch Tamara across the table from me as she eats a slice of garlic bread.

"Can we just be happy?" she asks. "We're together. We get to live together, and that's something."

I press my lips together, wanting to speak but holding back, knowing I must show restraint, not wanting to hurt them anymore by telling them what I really think. That they're quitters, that they've given up, that they're naive and fools to believe we will be rescued, that we're going to be here until we die, or until the people taking care of us die and we will never be found. That this dollhouse will be our graveyard.

"How'd they even build this place?" I ask. "I mean, who builds a whole apartment in a basement like this with no one finding out?"

Lindy shrugs. "I don't know, but I don't think those questions are going to help us. Let's just be grateful for what we have for tonight, at least, okay?"

The four of them look at me, pressing me to step in line. I pick up the canister of Parmesan cheese, sprinkling more on my pasta. "You're right. I don't need to complain about things that won't change."

Tamara beams at me. "Good," she says, "because your hair is so long and pretty, I want to see if I can do double French braids."

"Right," I say. "Sure. Of course."

I take another bite of meatball, feeling sick to my stomach, realizing if we're ever going to get out of here, it's going to be me who's going to hatch a plan.

These girls, they've been lost for far too long to think outside the box.

CHAPTER 17

Annie

Sitting down to eat dinner at a time like this feels completely inappropriate. How can I sit when my daughter is lost? When her backpack was just recovered?

I should be moving, doing something, but Emily finds me in the kitchen and tries to talk some sense into me.

"Mom," she says. "You need to eat. You need to take a break."

"I've been in the kitchen the whole afternoon," I tell her. "With Lisa and Susannah."

"I know, Mom, but they're gone now, and nothing's going to change in the next half an hour, whether or not you eat. You need to pause. You need to sit with us, with Dad. We need to remember that we're a family."

I look her in the eyes. "How are you being so strong and steady? Jubilee is gone, Emily. Our little girl." My shoulders shake, tears fill my eyes, as the truth of the last few days hits me.

"I know, Mom," she says, wrapping her arms around me. "But she's going to be found. It's going to be okay."

"You know how much I love her," I say.

"Of course, I do, Mom. We all love her and it's all going to be all right. She is going to be back home any minute, and we can go back to planning my wedding and focusing on happier things."

"How can you be so confident?" I ask.

She shrugs. "I have faith. Okay? I have faith that she'll be home before we know it. Remember when Josh was little, and he went out with a backpack and a sleeping bag? He said he was going to move to the woods."

"It's not the same, Emily. He lasted outside for about five hours before he realized he was hungry and hadn't packed any lemonade. It wasn't overnight."

Emily says, "Kids do stupid things. She wasn't thinking straight. Just because she's not here right now doesn't mean she's not coming back."

Josh, Andrew and Mason enter the house. David is behind them. James and Sarah are here, too.

"Okay," Sarah says, taking over. "The casseroles are here. There's plenty of food. We're going to sit down and eat a meal as family."

"Thank you," I say, giving Emily one last hug, wiping the tears from my eyes before walking over to my mother-in-law. "Thank you, too. Thank you, everyone. You are all being so strong, and all I'm doing today is crying."

My husband clears his throat. "Annie, it's all right. You can cry. It's a lot."

"Is the search party still out?" I ask.

David runs a hand over his jaw. "People are all taking a break right now to eat some food, which is what we're doing, too. Thankfully, we have great soon-to-be in-laws who brought us a meal."

He looks at Emily warmly. "I just saw Jaden," he tells me. "He's headed home."

Emily nods. "Yeah, that's what he said he was doing. I think he'll come back here later this evening."

"See?" David says, squeezing my hand. "Everyone's just going to take a break and we're going to eat some food, and it'll clear our heads so we can be more focused on finding Jubilee."

That puts everyone into action, reaching for plates and napkins and forks, scooping up the macaroni and cheese from the casserole dish, the pulled pork, and coleslaw. I'm thankful that we've been provided for so greatly today, but it's my heart that feels weary right now. I sit at the big dining room table with the rest of the family, but it's a somber mood. How can we laugh or make a joke or talk about our day when the only story we have to tell is one laced with worry?

James clears his throat. "Detective Montgomery seems like a good man."

David nods. "I agree. He was so patient with Annie and me earlier, explaining the protocol for missing children cases."

It's true, he was patient with me, especially considering that I was unable to focus on anything he was saying. I am grateful that David was able to take the lead in the brief conversation.

"Yeah, and he's been working lots of kidnapping cases in his career," Andrew says. "I think he knows what he is doing."

My eyebrows lift. "You spoke with the detective, too?"

He nods. "Yeah. I wanted to know if he was going to be able to do a good enough job to find my little sister. I wanted to make sure he had experience."

The smallest smile plays on my lips, and I look at my son with such adoration, with such care. For months, I have felt him pulling away, his teen angst getting in the way of us having a healthy relationship. But maybe this situation has pulled him out of his moodiness and helped him grow up. I blink away tears at the change in him.

"Why are you crying?" he asks, looking at me across the table.

I blink my eyes. "I don't know. I have so much to be grateful for, which sounds crazy considering Jubilee's not here, but I just love you all so much, and I know you all love her . . ."

"We do," Josh says. "She's my sister."

"How is Lisa holding up?" Sarah asks me.

"I think she was thankful to have a distraction today," I tell her.

"Their whole family was here for quite a while," James says.

I nod. "I don't think she wanted to go home. I think Jubilee being gone gave them all something to think about besides the fact that Leah is dead."

Mason stands. "Anybody want more milk?" He goes to get the gallon in the kitchen. There's a knock on the front door. "I'll get that," he says, already halfway there.

"Detective Montgomery," he says, pulling open the door and stepping aside. The detective enters our home. I feel more able to focus than the last time I saw him. Now I feel grounded, after sharing a meal with my family.

"What is it?" David asks, standing.

In a moment, I tense from head to toe. What if it's the worst possible news? What if the worst thing has happened? What if someone's been found? If she is . . . But I swallow my thoughts. I stand from the table with David, walking over to Montgomery.

"I wanted to talk to you about something that's been found," he tells us.

"What do you mean, 'been found'?" David asks.

The words *her body* enter my mind, but I don't want to think about that possibility.

"It's actually about Leah Monroe."

I frown. "You are here about Leah?"

Detective Montgomery nods. "Yes. Actually, is Josh here?"

I look over at my son sitting at the table. He stands. "I'm here." He walks over to us. "What is it?"

Montgomery looks past us at the rest of the table.

"It's fine," David says. "Say what you need to say. We're family here."

"The thing is, there was an arrowhead found in Leah's hand."

"An arrowhead?" David frowns. "What are you coming here to tell us that for?"

But I look at Josh. I know. Leah's mother mentioned that the arrowhead had been a gift from Josh, and it was the item she was holding when she was last alive.

"What are you insinuating?" David asks.

"The question I have," Detective Montgomery says, "is why Leah was holding that particular item before she took her last breaths, before she was murdered."

"Murdered," David said. "We're sure about that?"

The detective nods. "Yes. The head wounds were significant, according to the autopsy. She was killed in the cornfield, within the last week, maybe two."

I swallow, horrified. "So she's been held somewhere all this time?" For some reason, I had imagined her being dead for months. Not that she'd been alive all this time . . . and then, after months, someone wanted her dead? It feels worse, knowing this.

"So after months of captivity," Detective Montgomery says, "she managed to escape, or was released, and then she was killed. That's why it was so interesting, the discovery of the arrowhead."

"You can't prove it was Josh's," Andrew says, standing, clearly upset, coming to his brother's defense. "What are you trying to say? That you think my brother killed Leah, his best friend?"

"Nobody is saying that," Montgomery says. "But I'm going to need to bring you in for questioning, Josh."

Josh looks at David. "Dad, what should I do?"

"You're going to follow the detective's orders," David says. "His job is to find answers. I know you're innocent. You know you're innocent. That's what matters, son. You're going to do your best to tell anything you can to the detective to help find justice for Leah. That's what you can do for your best friend."

I look at my husband, appreciating his clear and decisive response. Josh is shaken, though, tears in his eyes. "I have to go to the police station?"

"That would be easiest," the detective says. "That way, we can record your statements and get them collected for evidence."

"Evidence? I didn't do anything. I didn't kill—"

"Honey," I say. "Nobody's saying you did anything. You're just going to tell them about the arrowhead. You're going to tell your side of the story."

"I don't have a side," he says. I gave her that for her fifteenth birthday because she's my—"

"I know, sweetie," I say.

David clears his throat. "You're going to do what the detective says, and then he is going to bring you home. All right? Would you like me to come with you?"

Josh shakes his head, looking back at the dinner table, his plate of food forgotten. His glass of milk never poured. "No, stay here, Dad. Find Jubilee. I will be back soon enough." He follows the detective out the front door, and I watch them walk away.

Then I look at David, my voice quivering. "It's going to be okay, right? Is everything going to be okay?"

And the first time in forever, when David looks back at me, his eyes searching mine, the confidence I usually have is gone.

When he looks at me, all I see is fear.

CHAPTER 18

Leah
Three months earlier

I can't stay in this apartment forever. After three months, that much is clear. And while the other four girls I'm living with don't seem quite as convinced that we could make our escape, I haven't given up hope.

In the bathroom, I whisper, "We need a plan." I spit out the toothpaste into the sink.

Tamara looks at me but doesn't speak. Her eyes flick up to the camera in the corner. It's creepy, that they are recording us even in here. We have no sense of privacy, and if I think about it too long, it makes me ill.

At breakfast, I pull out a notepad and a pen, and as I eat my granola and yogurt, I begin to write. The girls watch me as I quickly jot down some ideas in a bullet point.

> *Mutiny?*
> *Break the cameras?*
> *Throw her off guard?*

Tamara snatches the pad from me, ripping off the piece with my handwriting and crumpling up the sheet of paper. On the next blank sheet she writes, *Stop*.

Point taken, I think. I take another bite of granola and yogurt, wishing it didn't end there. Wanting a plan so bad, and not understanding why it's so hard to formulate one.

Except I know why: We are always all so groggy. Constantly yawning and rubbing our eyes, or needing to take a rest, napping in the afternoon, going to bed early and getting up late.

As the weeks have worn on, I know I've been sleeping more and more. As I think it, I yawn again, covering my mouth.

Lindy mentions it, too. "You're not the only one yawning," she says. "They must have upped the medication since you got here, because I'm sleeping way more than I used to."

Beth is literally sleeping at the table. An elbow props up her cheek, her eyes closed, and she sleeps with the yogurt untouched.

I'm scared in moments like this, because we're all so exhausted that we can't quite make any ideas come together. What kind of mutiny would we stage, anyway? Make a barricade against the wall with all the furniture in the apartment? Which they could use a sledgehammer to break down. And besides, it would only trap us in, not get us out.

But then, at least, I might get a chance to see them — her, him. The mother and father who are still unknown to me. We get letters from them every couple of days, tucked into the basket with our sandwiches for lunch or in the hamper where clean laundry is stacked with clean, folded dresses that arrive every few days, while we are sleeping.

I want to know who it is, who would've come and kidnapped me. If it's who I think it is, this is so much worse than I imagined.

But maybe I was entirely wrong, and the person I thought was the kidnapper wasn't.

But what would the coincidence of that be? To be kidnapped two days after sending an email accusing them of their crimes? It seems too unlikely.

Then again, it seems unrealistic that there is this underground dollhouse where five teenage girls are being held captive.

It feels like something out of a horror movie. A group of girls locked away, never to be seen again, growing old in their age. I shiver at my newest, most recent fear — that whoever Mother and Father are, they will come down here soon and take advantage of our bodies.

I clench my jaw, not wanting to think that way. But scared for all of us if they do. But considering we're prisoners, if they forced us to do anything, we'd have to obey.

The last item on my short list where I hoped to devise a plan is knocking her off her feet. Which means we have to stay awake long enough to intervene when she comes in.

And considering she watches those camera feeds, timing her entrances and exits perfectly with our sleep schedule, she never misses.

But we could pretend to sleep.

I grab the paper back from Tamara, the pen too, *pretend to sleep*, I write, wanting my words to be obvious, but facing them away from the camera.

I bow my head over the paper, wanting to conceal my letters, hoping it's not going to be seen on the footage.

Tamara looks at me and nods ever so gently. Feigning a cough to cover her lips as she speaks, she whispers, "We could try." The other girls nod.

"Today?" I ask.

They nod again.

It's not a perfect plan, but it's a start, and we need somewhere to begin if we're ever going to end this madness.

CHAPTER 19

Annie

After dinner, we all decide to leave the house, walking in pairs, to continue looking for Jubilee. The prevailing thought is that maybe there are places on the property where Jubilee is hiding, far more concealed than we thought. Maybe the police being here earlier today scared her, and she didn't dare reveal herself.

I'm with Emily, and as we're walking down the steps of the porch, Jaden pulls up in his police car.

"You don't have to go looking with me if you don't want," I say.

"No, Jaden can come with us," she says.

Jaden walks over to her and gives her a hug and a kiss on the cheek. "Hey," he says, "How is everyone holding up? I heard Detective Montgomery came for Josh."

"He came over during dinner. It was completely unexpected," I say. "David and James are out back. Everybody's doing another walkthrough. I guess the police are starting a more thorough search tomorrow, since we'll have passed the twenty-four-hour mark."

Jaden nods. "Yeah, I was just coming here to tell you guys about that."

"Well, we're hoping to find her tonight," Emily says. "I bet she's just hiding somewhere really well on the property, not wanting to be found. You know how kids are."

Jaden, though, doesn't confirm her optimism. "I want to believe that," he says.

"Well, you don't think anything has to do with Josh, do you?" Emily asks, her voice tight.

"Jubilee?" Jaden asks. He shakes his head. "No, not at all."

"But what about Leah?" I ask, hating that I even voiced the question. I don't think Josh is capable of anything cruel, but the arrowhead spooked me in a way that makes me feel ashamed.

"The thing is," Jaden says, "There have been five other girls gone missing in this county the last ten years. If Jubilee is number six . . ."

"Five others?" Emily says. "That seems a lot. "

"The only reason Josh is connected to any of this is he was alone the with her the night she disappeared. Lisa said they were being inappropriate in the backyard."

"Inappropriate how?" I ask, stunned.

Jaden exhales. "It's not my place to say, but they were in an embrace."

"Well, they were best friends. What is Lisa getting at?"

Jaden blows air from his cheeks. "Look, it was out of line for me to even say that."

I am more concerned with the missing girls. "If there were five girls that have gone missing over the last ten years," I say, "how does that statistic differ from other counties in that time span? It doesn't seem like that big of a number, all things considered."

"You're right," Jaden says, "maybe it's not. But I know it's not connected to Josh in any way whatsoever. "

"You really think Jubilee might have been girl number six?" I ask, stunned that my daughter might not be coming back. The idea of her being found dead hadn't felt real. But now, with Jaden standing here in his police uniform, putting these ideas in my head, I am questioning everything.

David and James walk over to us then. "Jaden," David says. "Good to see you again."

"Of course," he says. "I heard about Josh."

David nods. "I'm sure he'll be back any moment. They couldn't be questioning him about too much."

"Jaden was just telling me about other girls who have gone missing," I say.

"That over the last ten years, there's been four other girls in Thomas County who've gone missing. Leah added to that makes it five. One of them was over in Pritchard."

"I remember that," David says.

"In Pritchard?" I say.

"What year was that?" James asks.

"Four years ago," Jaden says.

I frown. "You were doing a build over there that time, weren't you? That subdivision?"

David nods. "Yeah. We were out there for three years working. I remember when it happened, because we were interviewed."

I frown. "You were interviewed about a missing girl?"

"Yeah."

"Why didn't you tell me?"

"Annie, of course I told you. But it was years ago."

"I see," I say. "So you didn't know anything about it?"

"Of course not," David says. "I only came out there to do a job. Day work. James was with me, the whole crew."

James nods. "Don't you think it's pretty soon to be drawing correlations between those girls who have gone missing over the years, throughout the whole county, with Jubilee, who hasn't even been missing for a day? Not to mention Jubilee's history with running away."

David reaches for my hand. "I agree with Dad. Jubilee has gone through so much, Leah being found probably triggered something. She's got to be around here somewhere. I think we just hold on to faith for a little bit longer, Annie. I don't think we should get this distorted, thinking it's bigger than it is. We shouldn't blow it out of proportion."

It's impossible to hold back my tears. "But our girl is gone, David."

He pulls me close, giving me the tight hug I need, grounding me so I don't wash away in my emotions. "I know. That is why we are going to find her and bring her home."

CHAPTER 20

Jubilee
Two months earlier

Sunday dinners here are like make-believe. I'm not exaggerating when I say that. Nothing about it seems like real life. At least not a real life I've ever known.

We have dinner together, and Grandma and Grandpa come around. And then afterwards, we go to the living room. We sit around the coffee table, and someone pulls out the iPad, and they call Elijah — Annie and David's oldest son. My big brother, I guess.

He's in the Army, but he always stops whatever he's doing, if he's out with friends or having dinner or playing Ultimate Frisbee. He always stops, answers the phone, and he talks to all of us, every last one. Emily and Mason and Josh and Andrew and Annie and David and Grandpa James and Grandma Sarah, and me even. Me, a girl he doesn't even know.

Elijah's a big guy. He's strong and looks like he could fight a bear. Probably a good thing that he's in the Army. I've never known someone like him.

But really, I've never known someone like anybody in this house. It's sure different from my last foster home.

There, I could do whatever I wanted. Sometimes I miss that. Maybe it's bad to say that, but it's the truth. I miss knowing I could stay up as late as I wanted without anybody noticing, or watching TV all day if I felt like it, or just running away and nobody noticing for a while.

Here, everyone seems to know what I'm doing all of the time. Sometimes, it feels a little tight around my body, like a hug that's too close, too long. And I want to push it away, all this goodness. Because it feels too much, like I don't deserve it.

Annie says everybody deserves love, but Annie wouldn't understand because she's not like me. She's always been in a family like this.

I tell her as much when she tucks me into bed after FaceTime on Sunday night. Everybody's in a good mood because Elijah just got promoted or something in the Army. He got a new badge and more money.

"Maybe I could be in the Army someday," I say to Annie.

She smiles, sitting on the edge of my bed and tucking me in. "Would you like that?"

I shrug. "Well, everyone seems to like the fact that Elijah does it."

"Well, that was Elijah's dream for a lot of years. When he was growing up, he would talk about wanting to be in the service, protect our country and put his skills to good use. We all had different talents, different skills."

"Like Grandma Sarah, she's good at making dresses," I say, and Annie nods. "And like David. He's good at making houses." Annie nods again. "What about you, Annie? What do you do for your job?" I frown, realizing she never really is apart from me.

"Well, I'm your mom. I'm everybody's mom here. That's my job."

I twist my lips. "Sarah, though, she sells her dresses, doesn't she? At some stores downtown?"

Annie nods, "Yes, she does. Aprons, and quilts — she sells lots of different things. And she goes to craft bazaars a lot in the winter."

"Do you want to do that?" I ask her. "Have a job like that, sell things or make things or do things besides cleaning and cooking?"

Annie's smile gets tighter. "Oh, well, I do lots of other things. I homeschool everybody, and I made sure you took a shower and that your tangles were all combed out of your hair," she says. Her voice is light, but her eyes aren't quite as bright as her voice sounds.

I bite my bottom lip. "Are you upset with me?"

"Of course not," she says quickly. "Of course you didn't upset me. I love being a mother. I love taking care of everybody here, being a good wife and a good daughter-in-law."

"Where's your family, though?" I ask her, realizing for the first time since I've ever been home that I actually know nothing about her side of the family. "Grandma and Grandpa are David's parents. Where's your mom and dad?"

"We don't see them," she says.

"Why not? Where do they live?"

"They live far from here," she says, her voice now high-pitched, like she is trying hard to keep her words even. "They live in Wyoming. That's where I grew up, and we're not in contact with them anymore."

"Why not?"

"Well, Jubilee, not all parents do a good job at taking care of other people in the family. Kind of like . . . remember how it was for you when you were younger, with your birth mom and dad?"

"Do you mean how they left me at the birthday party?"

Annie nods. "Yeah, like that."

I shrug. "Well, my counselor says they didn't know what they were doing because they're probably not well."

Annie presses her lips together. "And what do you think about that?"

I push my lips out, thinking. "I think that day at the party was the worst day of my life. But you know what the best day of my life was?"

"What's that?" Annie asks.

"Coming here. The day you and David brought me home in that van and drove me up to the farmhouse for the very first time, and I saw everybody out on the porch waiting for me, that was the best day ever. It made up for all those bad days."

"Were there a lot of bad days?" Annie asks me.

I swallow. "Yeah, there were a lot of bad days. At the foster home, mostly, but before that, too. I guess there had always been bad days."

"I understand what you mean," Annie says. Her voice is soft now. It's mostly a whisper. And she runs her hand over my hair, tucking a strand behind my ear.

"Are you crying?" I ask her.

She blinks quickly. "There were a lot of bad days before I met your dad, David, before we got married and moved into this farmhouse. There was a lot of time in my life where I thought I was always going to be alone, too. Where I thought my heart would never be whole."

"And now it is?" I ask her. "Whole, I mean."

She smiles. "More whole than I ever imagined. Now, I have you, Jubilee."

I can't help but smile at that. I giggle, too. "I'm the reason your heart's whole?"

She nods. "Yes. Yes, it is."

"Do you think a whole heart could have a break again?" I ask her.

She frowns, tilting her head, looking at me like the question I asked is confusing. "I mean, I suppose. Hearts are breakable things, fragile things."

"I heard a heart gets stronger the more you use it."

Annie smiles. "Where'd you hear that?"

"I don't know. Maybe my counselor."

"Well, she sounds like she's probably a smart lady."

"She was," I say, with a laugh. "You think that's true? The way a heart works?"

Annie nods. "I may not have a job outside of the house, I may not get paid for the work I do, but," she says, "I do know a thing or two about hearts, about love. And I know this, Jubilee: I know that I love you."

CHAPTER 21

Annie

When I get into bed, I'm exhausted. David is already snoring by the time I pull the covers up over my body, and I'm desperate to fall asleep as well, to fade into some sort of dream, not wanting the nightmare of the day to haunt me any longer.

But sleep doesn't come. I'm restless. And even though my bones themselves feel heavy, the weight in my chest is heavier still. Maybe it's the mother's cry within me, a desperate plea to the universe or to the heavens for my little girl to be returned to me now.

The gift of her in our life was so beautiful, so perfectly orchestrated, even me bringing up the subject of adoption to David, a conversation I anticipated being one where I was convincing him, went smoothly. He knows me better than anyone and understood that having another child would give me a sense of purpose. And it has.

All along the way, through the adoption steps and getting licensed to be a foster parent for her, getting her room ready and making our home ready for a little girl, those things kept me busy in ways I haven't been in so long, with the other kids getting so much older.

I don't know why my mind is reliving those moments leading up to bringing her home, because all they are seeming to do is confirm how very much I longed for her and prepared our lives for her.

The idea, that after all of this I've let her down, is untenable. She must be found. She must be. There's no way around it. But in this exact moment, it seems so far off because it wasn't just our family searching for her today. The police department of Thomas County was here. The sheriff and the deputy, Detective Montgomery — everyone was looking.

When they brought me news that her backpack had been found in the woods, all I wanted to know was what was inside of it. An officer read me the list of what was found in the pack, telling me I couldn't go through it myself because it was collected for evidence.

Evidence? My daughter's blue backpack is evidence? It doesn't feel real.

I roll over on my side, my back facing David. I tuck a pillow under my head, closing my eyes, wanting to sleep. But instead of counting sheep, I count the items that were in the bag. Three granola bars, four juice boxes, one box of markers, one notepad, a pair of jeans, a sweatshirt, four hair clips. She was planning to be gone. I know enough about how kids operate. She had food. She had clothes. She had a plan.

This reality doesn't help things. It just makes it feel all that much worse.

She wanted to go. She wanted to leave us, but why? There had been no major blowups besides getting frustrated when she was stealing food or hiding in the house. My chest seizes. Did we look everywhere inside this house?

"David," I say, rolling over and shaking his shoulder, "we should look in the house again. Did you go through the basement and the attic?"

"Annie, we looked everywhere. The police searched the house, too."

"When?" I ask. "I've been here all day. I didn't remember anyone going up to the attic."

"You were probably in the kitchen, honey. Everyone looked through the house."

"You sure? What if she's under this roof?"

"That would be a miracle, but it's not possible, Annie," he says. He rolls back over and within minutes, he's sleeping, his shoulders heaving, his breath heavy. I get out of bed and push my feet into my slippers, reaching for the bathrobe on the chair next to my nightstand. I tie it around my waist and walk down to the living room.

I have a small desk in a corner where I've always filed our bills and kept track of our homeschool curriculum. There's a bookshelf with the supplies I use to make sure all the kids have kept on track for their yearly studies. My laptop is here, too, and I lift the lid, typing in my password. I see I have missed dozens of Facebook messages, notifications, people wondering about Jubilee, having heard that she's gone. I instantly regret opening the page.

While I had acknowledged the texts I received throughout the day, I hadn't checked any of my social media, and I have no interest in doing so now.

I click out of Facebook and instead type in the *Thomas County Newspaper* web address. From there, I use the search feature. Missing girl, local. Dozens of articles pop up, and I begin to sort through them, starting from the end.

Ever since Jaden mentioned the other girls who had gone missing in Thomas County over the last several years, I've wanted to see what I could find out on my own.

It takes me a while to scroll through article after article. By the time I finish reading, my eyes feel bloodshot, my faith in humanity weakening.

Tamara was nine years old when she went missing, ten years ago, from Eaton.

Lindy was ten seven years ago, when she went missing from Battle Point, my town.

Four years ago, Carrie, age eight, from Oakdale, was last seen at a carnival in Pritchard.

Two years ago, Beth, also ten years old, was out for a walk headed to the library. She was never seen again.

Six months ago, it was Leah, fifteen years old.

And now, I wonder if Jubilee is added to this list.

Are the missing girls being taken by same person? Is any of this connected in any way?

I don't know which would be better, or what would be worse. Of course, I don't like the idea of a serial kidnapper turned murderer in Thomas County, but I also don't like the idea of my little girl lost, never to be found. And if all the other girls were younger, why deviate and kidnap Leah, a fifteen-year-old?

"Mom?"

I turn around. "What is it?" I ask. Josh's there, standing in the shadows.

"Hey, what you looking at?" he asks, stepping toward me. I close the computer, not wanting him to be reminded that Leah's gone. I don't want him to see the articles that are covering my laptop screen documenting the girls who've gone missing over the years.

I rub my eyes. "You should be asleep."

"I know, but I can't. I just keep thinking about being at the police station, being interrogated like that. I really wasn't expecting . . ." His shoulders begin to shake, and I stand from my chair, wrapping my arms around my boy who's nearly grown.

"Oh, Josh," I say. "It's okay. You can cry now. I'm here. Mom is here." And I am. And I hold him tight and he cries against me. He's a full head taller than I am, but that doesn't matter in moments like this. A mother's love, a mother's hug, transcends height.

"It's like they thought I did something to her," he says. "It was her birthday, you know, the night she was taken or she left or whatever."

"I know, honey," I say.

"And it was funny because we were at their house for dinner, right? Remember? And she told me to come outside with her. But first we went in her room because she wanted to show me something."

We move to the couch in the living room, and I keep my mouth shut, just wanting him to express everything he has kept bottled up.

"And she had this box of all these things from when we were little: this origami crane, a scrap of paper where we played the game MASH. Remember how we used to play that? She was going to live in a mansion with Justin Bieber." Josh smiles, wiping his eyes. "There were these bracelets we made at church camp when we were in middle school, and there was a $500 Monopoly bill."

"What was that about?" I ask him.

He smiles. "Well, Monopoly was always her favorite, and we said one day we'd be rich. We'd have $500 bills ourselves, and we promised that we would take each other out for dinner in Seattle at the Space Needle. I'll never get to do that now, Mom. And the thing is, I have $500 in my bank. I saved it from working for Grandpa last summer. I should've just taken her for her birthday. Why did I wait? Now, I'll never get the chance to take her to that dinner. She'll never get the chance to . . ." Josh starts crying again. "And I told that to the detective. I explained to him everything in that box, and they said they had the box. But nothing about that box and what is in it means anything to anyone but Leah and me."

"Was that everything you talked to the detective about? What about the arrowhead?"

Josh wipes his eyes, then musters the strength to keep talking. "Then we went outside, Leah and me, and I gave her another birthday gift. You know how in church sometimes people talk about promise rings?"

I frown, not expecting this turn of conversation. A promise ring is a pre-engagement ring . . . it is not my favorite tradition, and I am shocked that Josh would do something like that before discussing it with David and me. After all, he is only fifteen. "You gave her a promise ring because you planned to marry her one day?"

He shakes his head. "No, I knew her parents wouldn't like that. I gave her the arrowhead as a promise. A promise she would understand."

I nod, only slightly relieved. "I remember the arrowhead. We went to that Whitman Museum and saw all the Native American artifacts."

"I still had mine after all that time," he says. "And Mom, you know what?"

"What, honey?" I ask, pressing a hand to my heart, amazed at both his decision to confide in me and that he had so much love for Leah. I didn't realize the depth of it. I knew they were friends, but they had talked of marriage. No wonder he has been so utterly heartbroken the last six months. It was more than his best friend who was gone, it was his first love. It makes me wonder about the depths of the emotions all of us hide from one another, the pain we bury or the masks we wear.

"She kissed me," he tells me. "That night on her birthday, you guys were all inside, and they were going to have the cake any minute. We went outside to that swing set they had in the backyard. I had never kissed anybody before. Neither had she. She was my best friend, but she was more than that, Mom."

"I know, sweetheart."

"And she kissed me. And then she kissed that arrowhead and she put it in her pocket, and we went back inside."

My heart aches for my son, the loss he must feel right now is monumental. And even though I have been consumed with Jubilee, I know Leah weighs ever so heavy on his heart, and with good reason. "Thank you for sharing those memories with me," I say to him. "They're beautiful."

"They're also pretty sad, Mom."

"It's okay for them to be sad," I tell him. "It doesn't take away any of the significance."

"The detective listened to me. I told him most of that, too. Well, all of it, even though I didn't want to tell him about the kiss, but I did. And you know what he said? He told me he appreciated my honesty. He wasn't mean to me or anything."

"I didn't think he was going to be, honey."

"I didn't know," Josh says. "I've never been to a police station before. But it sucks, because it's not like I told them anything that was going to change the fact that Leah is gone, and somebody killed her."

"Well, they ruled you out. That's something."

Josh's eyes turned dark. "It's horrible. Whoever did this to her, and whoever took Jubilee, needs to pay."

I pull in a sharp breath. "Is that what you think has happened? Someone took your sister?"

He nods. "I know someone took her."

"How can you be so sure?"

"Because Jubilee may have had a short temper, but she loved us. Mom, she loved you."

CHAPTER 22

Leah
Three months earlier

We close our eyes, we lie down, but we've made a promise that we're not going to fall asleep, not this afternoon. We want to see Mother when she comes in.

I want to look into her eyes and make a plan, a real plan, a game plan to get the hell out of here.

I close my eyes. I tell myself a story, wanting to stay awake. Instead of counting sheep, I tell myself a story of escape, of me knocking down the doors, of me getting back outside into the fresh air and taking a lungful and letting it out. And looking up into the sky and seeing the sun, the clouds, the blue.

I want to stay awake. I want to. I want to . . . My breathing grows shallow.

I wake with a start, sitting upright in bed. I look around. I know the time has passed because the clock on the bedside table says 3:30. It's been two hours since I got into bed.

Next to the clock is a bouquet of daisies. They weren't there when I lay down with the intention of feigning sleep.

It didn't work. The meds they give us are just too strong to fight against.

I close my eyes again, rolling over, pressing my face into the pillow and screaming as loud as I can. I scream again and again and again, and my sisters wake and they're annoyed, asking, "What are you doing? Be quiet."

But I don't care. I don't care anymore. I've got to get out of here, and I'm not going to pretend to sleep. No, I'm going to do something bigger, something bolder, something more brave.

This is my one life, and I'm getting out of here alive if it's the last thing I do.

CHAPTER 23

Annie

After I get Josh to go back to bed, I re-scan the articles on my laptop. It's late, 3:00 a.m., and I know I should be asleep, but something is nagging at me that I can't seem to shake. I look back at the girls who've gone missing, and the cities where they lived, and the dates. I remember how yesterday David and James mentioned that they had been working in Pritchard when Beth had gone missing, that they had even been interviewed about it, because they'd been at a job site not far from where she was taken.

As I look at the dates of the other girls, I go back in my emails, checking some of the jobs that David did over the years, projects he was a part of. I'm not sure why I feel compelled to cross-check these things, but something about it doesn't feel right. I would've remembered if there had been a girl that had gone missing in Pritchard and that David had been interviewed about it. It's not that I'm questioning his honesty; it's more my own memory.

And when I go back in time, I realize that ten years ago, when Tamara was taken in Monroe, David had been doing a custom build for an attorney out there. Nine years ago in

Battle Point, when Lindy was abducted, he'd been working on a summer house on a lake. When Carrie was taken six years ago from Oakdale, David and James had been there too, working on a subdivision. The success they'd had with that one is what brought them to Pritchard a few years later, when Beth went missing. Of course, Leah was taken from here in Battle Point — where David and I live.

And I don't know why any of this even feels significant, why I feel the need to even look these projects up and compare them to the years the girls were taken. But my instinct, my gut feeling, led me to do it. But why? I close my computer, feeling sick to my stomach, not liking any of what I've connected. And is it a connection or a coincidence?

Months after that job in Monroe, David was working somewhere else. David and James have been working all over this county for years, decades, and there are bigger coincidences in life than this. Besides, what am I trying to connect here? That my own husband has something to do with any of this? That's grotesque and absurd, and honestly, wildly inappropriate.

I hate that I even let these intrusive thoughts enter my mind. With the computer closed, I walk down the hall to Jubilee's room. I step inside and crawl into her bed. It's a narrow twin mattress and I roll to my side, looking out the window. The curtains are pulled back, and I can see the moon heavy in the sky through it. I wonder, wherever she is, if she's looking at that same moon, if she has a view of the heavens and the earth.

But I don't know where she is. I don't know if she's safe and I don't know if she can see the moon, let alone the stars. I close my eyes, holding onto the hope that just maybe, she can. I whisper a prayer to her, hoping that she can hear it somehow. The cry of a mother's heart.

I love you, Jubilee. I won't stop until I find you. I chose you, and I would choose you all over again. You're more than the sun, you're my moon and my stars. And I love you like I've known you forever.

I wake in the morning with a start. I hear the boys up in the living room and someone in the kitchen, coffee brewing, and I sit up from the bed, rubbing my eyes and looking around Jubilee's bedroom.

I have no idea what's happened to those other girls that I was looking into last night, but as I wake to a new day, I know one thing for certain: I'm finding my daughter.

I push back the covers and make the bed before walking to the kitchen to join the rest of my family. Emily pours me a cup of coffee, and I reach for it, adding half-and-half, thanking her. "You get enough rest, Mom?"

I nod. "I did."

She looks at me as though she doesn't believe me. I'm sure my eyes are bloodshot from the tears and exhaustion. And I look over at David, who is eating a container of yogurt. "How'd you sleep?" I ask him.

"All right," he says. "It's early, but the police and the detective should be out here soon. I want to be up and going when they get here."

I nod. "I'm going to take a quick shower and then I'll join you outside."

"Morning, boys," I say, looking at Mason, Josh and Andrew. "Has anyone gotten a chance to talk to Elijah?" I ask.

David nods. "Yeah, I spoke with him yesterday."

"Good," I say, glad they are able to keep their brother updated.

"Why don't you go take a shower?" David says. "You'll feel better once you do."

He's right. Twenty minutes later, I'm dressed and clean, ready for the day. I quickly blow dry my hair before tying it back with an elastic, lacing my tennis shoes, wanting to be dressed to go outside and actually do my part in searching for Jubilee.

I can't spend another day in this house, wringing my hands, praying she comes back. I need to actually search for her until she's found, because I can't trust anybody else to do that.

After all, these officers were all looking into the other girls who were never found. How can I have faith that anyone can help me, when no one helped those families? Not in a way that brought anybody justice, that brought anybody home.

After I'm ready for the day, I walk outside with a new cup of coffee. I see that Detective Montgomery is here, standing with a group of officers, and there are about twenty-five people gathered in the yard.

I stand back, listening as Detective Montgomery explains the situation. "Jubilee has been missing for over twenty-four hours. This means we are going to be working around the clock until we bring her home. There will be no rest, no reprieve. The one and only goal at this moment is to bring her home safely. I'm thankful that everyone who's been able to come out today is willing to do their part in searching. And although we looked at the premises yesterday, we are going to be expanding our parameters. We have an office on wheels in the driveway, and if you head that way, you can be assigned a location. It's most important that you have a buddy. Working together is the most efficient way to cover the ground. If you have any questions, ask any officer you see. Our job is to help, our job is to find Jubilee. Now, thank you again, and good luck."

Montgomery ends his speech and then walks over toward David. I join them. David wraps an arm around my shoulder. "Any other updates on Jubilee?" David asks Montgomery.

"As of now, no. But we are doing everything we can. I know that's not what you want to hear, but it's all I have to offer at this moment. But it's early in the day, it's only 7:30, which means we have plenty of time to work in daylight."

Montgomery walks away and I look at David. His eyes search mine. "Josh says you were up in the middle of the night on the computer. What were you looking for?"

I rub my temples with my fingers. I want to be honest, but I don't want to open a can of worms either. "I was looking up the other girls that had gone missing in the county. After Jaden mentioned that last night, I couldn't shake it."

"Why?" David says. "Those girls aren't our girl."

"I know, but it's strange, isn't it?" I take a sharp breath, knowing the best way forward is to be direct. My only aim is to find my daughter. "And do you know what's even more strange? I was looking at the dates of the girls who were abducted and in the different cities around the county, it was the same time that you were doing builds."

He frowns. "What do you mean?"

"I mean, like that girl Tamara, ten years ago, she was taken from Monroe and that's when you were working out there. Same thing about Oakdale and Pritchard and Battle Point and . . ."

David frowns. "Wait, what are you insinuating?"

"Nothing. It's just weird, right? I just mean, out of all the places you could have been . . . it's weird."

"I'm trying not to get upset here, Annie. I'm trying to track with where you're going with this. But are you accusing me of something? Of something beyond the pale?"

"No," I say slowly. "I don't even know why I said it. I'm not meaning anything. It just seemed strange. And they said you were interviewed, and I never remember you telling me about that."

He scoffs. "Annie, I know you're looking for an answer, but pinning this on your husband?"

"I'm not pinning anything on you. I was in bed with you the night Jubilee left the house. I know you were here. I'm not saying anything."

Except I wasn't, was I?

I got ready for bed that night, and David told me he needed to take care of some things in the office. I went to sleep; he left the room. Where did he really go?

"Then what are you doing bringing up these other girls, connecting them to me and my crew?" David asks.

"I don't know. It just seems strange, is all."

"And what's really strange," he says, "is that right now you're somehow trying to bring division between us, when what we need to be doing is staying more tightly together than we ever had before. Annie, I love you and I love our family and I'm not losing any of it, any of us. Okay? So don't let your mind go to these dark places. I know you have a tendency of catastrophizing things, but this is not a catastrophe. I'm not some criminal who's been kidnapping girls for the last decade."

"I know," I say. "I wasn't saying that. It's just it was weird, and I noticed the dots connecting."

"They didn't connect. It was just circumstantial coincidence."

I swallow. "I know," I say. And I do. Logically, I know everything David is saying is true.

But then, why does it all feel so off?

CHAPTER 24

Jubilee
One month ago

I think Mom's upset with me. She says she's not, but I feel it, and it's all my fault because I keep messing things up.

She doesn't like it when I take the food from the cupboard and hide it in my bedroom or put the leftovers from my plate in my pockets. I'm not doing it to be mean or sneaky. I'm doing it because I can't help myself. It's something I've been doing for as long as I can remember, and it's embarrassing when I get caught.

I hate it when she pulls up my mattress and sees a peanut-butter-and-jelly sandwich underneath it. Or when she's doing my laundry and goes through my clothes and finds empty wrappers of food I took without permission. She says in this house there is no such thing as permission when it comes to food. She says there's no lock on the pantry, that I can have any food anytime I want, and the fridge is open for me anytime also and that I can have as much as I want, and I don't need to take it and hide it. And I don't mean to, but still, I do.

Now she's sitting at the kitchen table with Susannah, her best friend. They're drinking coffee. When Susannah comes over, they sit at the kitchen table with coffee and they eat something sweet. Today, it's blueberry muffins that Susannah brought.

"I love the crumble topping," Mom says.

"Thanks," Susannah says smiling. They see me standing in the doorway. "Did you want one?" Susannah asks.

"Sure. If I can?" I ask Mom, looking at her.

She exhales slowly as if this statement is annoying, and I realize it is.

"Jubilee, Susannah offered you a muffin. Of course you can have a muffin. Like I said so many times before, you are free to eat anything in the house that you want at any time. There are no restrictions of food in our home. Okay? That goes for everyone who lives here."

Susannah presses her lips together but doesn't add anything to the conversation.

"Thanks, Susannah," I say, taking one off the plate on the kitchen counter and reaching for a paper napkin.

"Why don't you go eat that on the front porch?" Mom suggests.

"All right," I say. I walk out of the kitchen, but I don't get out of earshot. Just out of their sight. I want to hear what they're talking about. I want to know if, when I walk away, if Mom is going to start talking about me, saying all the reasons she doesn't love me or want me.

"So, how are things going?" Susannah asks her. "I mean, really."

"With Jubilee?" Mom asks. I can hear her sigh. Her voice lowered. "Jubilee is wonderful. She really is such a sweetheart. But sometimes I feel over my head, the things she struggles with, the life she's lived . . . And I'm saying that as someone coming from a hard place, too. My childhood was a mess, you know that."

"From what you've shared," Susannah says, "I do. But I guess it was a different kind of mess?"

"Exactly," Mom says. "Jubilee's emotions are like a rollercoaster. Most days, I don't know if she's going to be happy or sad or angry. And the stuff with the food and the lying, sometimes she just shuts down altogether."

"Is she in therapy?"

"Yes. We've set her up with someone, but it's through our insurance, and it's a little clunky getting the appointments scheduled consistently. I wish she could keep seeing the person she saw back with the foster family, because she'd been seeing that woman for about fourteen months. It's a lot of new."

These words make my insides get tight and crumpled up, and I take a bite of the muffin that's in my hand. And then another and another. I want to hear what she's saying, but I also don't want to think about it.

"Well, I'm glad she's in therapy. What about you, Annie? How are you taking care of yourself? Because you know Jubilee's going to be dealing with these things for a long time. What she needs is a mom who is devoted to really meeting her needs."

"I am doing my best to take care of myself. I am."

"How?" Susannah asks. "What are you doing for you?"

"Gosh, you say it like . . . I don't know, like I am doing something wrong."

"I'm not saying you're doing anything wrong," Susannah says gently, "but everything I always hear is that we need to put ourselves first. Not in a selfish way, but in a way to fill our cup, so we can fill up other people's."

"What are you doing for yourself?" Mom asks her.

"Currently, I am going to that Pilates studio downtown, and I've been trying a lot of new recipes, baking a lot, cooking."

"Well, I cook all the time, too."

"I know, and you've always been a great cook. Look, all I'm saying is you are giving so much to your family, to Jubilee. Maybe you need to give something to you."

"That's easy for you to say."

"Why?" Susannah says. "Because I only have one child and you have five? I don't think that's very fair."

"I wasn't meaning it like that," Mom says.

"Then how are you meaning it?" Susannah presses.

"I don't know. You're right. It is judging you and your life in ways that aren't fair. I'm sorry."

"It's okay," Susannah says. "You know I would've had more children if I could. And it's not like going to Pilates every day is what I wanted to do with my life, but life happens in ways we didn't plan."

"And how are Terry and Nathan doing?" Mom ask her.

"They are doing okay. Nathan is so busy right now. He is taking some classes at the community college, and he got a job at the sports store in town. Terry has his practice, and he just hired some new staff. I have more free time than ever before."

"Sounds nice," Mom says. "Maybe I should come to Pilates with you sometime, get out of the house."

"Anytime," Susannah says. "You know I always have time for you."

I walk to the front porch, feeling unsettled, thinking maybe Mom loves me but that she isn't happy. And maybe it's the kind of unhappy that has nothing to do with me.

CHAPTER 25

Annie

I know I've upset David, but this whole thing is upsetting me. I look at him in confusion.

"Okay, I'm sorry. You're right. It wasn't appropriate. I don't know what I was even saying that for, or even *thinking* that for, and it's all messy and complicated, David, but I feel like nothing is going on with finding Jubilee. We're not any closer to finding our daughter than we were yesterday morning at this time. Do you actually believe that Detective Montgomery has the ability to find her? Because the crazy thing to me is, all those other girls that have gone missing, none of them came home. And Leah was just found dead."

"Annie," he says, "You've got to get a grip."

"Do I? A grip on what?"

"The situation. Look, let's go tell Montgomery we need an update."

I look at my husband with frustration. "He literally just told us, David, that there is no update."

"Maybe he's saying that to avoid getting our hopes up. We're the parents of the missing child. We deserve more information."

At this moment, I feel a surge of gratitude towards him for taking control. I need him to be taking the lead in this moment, because I feel like I'm falling apart, and I'm so thankful he is staying strong. I take his hand.

"I love you," I say.

"I love you more."

Together, we walk over to Detective Montgomery, who appears to be briefing some other officers.

"Excuse me. Can we have a word?" David asks him.

The other officers walk away, leaving Detective Montgomery with us.

"I know you just told us that there was no information, but that's not enough right now. We need more than *we're looking*."

"I don't know what you want me to tell you," Montgomery says. He has closely cropped black hair and is wearing a dark navy suit with an olive-green tie.

As I look him over, I realize he's wearing the same clothes from yesterday, and he has a five o'clock shadow at 7:30 in the morning. My heart goes out to him as I realize why he looks this way. He's been working around the clock for us, for our family.

"It's okay," I say, "we know you're doing everything you can. We're not trying to add more pressure."

His shoulders fall ever so slightly. "Thank you for saying that. We really are doing our best. It's a difficult situation when we're working on a case like this. Giving false hope to a family isn't in anyone's best interests, but I want you to know that we are working on a few things. We've checked the bus stations. All the cameras from the one in Thomas County showed no signs of Jubilee. We are now working on footage of local gas stations. We wouldn't be able to determine if she was picked up by a hitchhiker, of course, but we are looking at footage from every camera we can, any intersections and highway cameras. If we notice something that is out of the ordinary, we will run with it. Beyond that, we sent her backpack to the labs, to see if there were any fingerprints that could be picked up."

"Were there?" I ask.

"I'm sure you can imagine what I was thinking when I saw that bag," Montgomery says. "Maybe she hadn't dropped it, maybe someone had left it behind, someone whose hands had grasped it."

I swallow, the idea of that so horrific.

But my fears are settled when Montgomery adds, "But there were no prints, Annie, David. This is what I didn't want to say, because we've come to a few dead ends, and that just means there's less for you to hold onto. And right now, the most important thing you can do for Jubilee is hold on to hope. You are her family; you are the ones who know her best. You're the ones who might remember something, think of something, that can give us a clue forward."

"Wait," I say. "What about her old foster family? Has anyone looked there?"

"Annie," David says, "that was all the way out on the coast in Grace Harbor."

"I know," I say. "But what if she was trying to make her way there?"

"That's a three-hour drive. How would she do that on foot?" he asks.

"Maybe she got picked up by a hitchhiker. I don't know."

Detective Montgomery nods. "No, this is good, Annie. We can go off of that, and maybe it'll take us somewhere."

I exhale, feeling a sense of purpose. "Of course," I say. "I can get you their contact information. I have it all in our files."

"Great," Montgomery says. "I'll assign an officer to help you with that. This is what I'm talking about, having faith. Not getting upset over things not coming together with this case, but having trust that eventually they will. We will find Jubilee."

"I know," I say, feeling shaky with fear. "I'm just scared that when we find her, it might be too late."

* * *

After lunchtime, I get a text from Susannah. *Leah's memorial service is in two days at 10:00 a.m. I thought you would want to know.*

I type out a quick reply. *Have you seen Lisa? Just wondering if she's come down from her high of yesterday.*

My phone rings. It's Susannah, checking in. "How's the search going today? Terry is still out there."

"I don't know," I admit. "It's really hard to get a good pulse on any of it. It's not like anyone's around the house. Everyone's out looking. I was too, all morning, but it's exhausting, covering the ground and just hoping that she might be somewhere, anywhere. Around the next corner, around the next tree line, around the next hill." I pull in a sharp breath, stifling a sob.

"Oh, sweetie." Susannah says, "Do you want me to come over? I was just on my way out of the house. I'm going to bring some food over to Lisa's."

"Can I come with you?" I ask her.

"You sure?"

"Yeah, I need to breathe for a second. It feels claustrophobic here."

"Of course," Susannah says. "I'll be there in a few minutes. How about I bring Nathan with me and he can hang out with Josh for a few hours? Might be good for the boys."

I exhale with relief at the offer. "Josh has been pacing the property. A good friend coming over will help with his anxiety; at least I hope it will."

"Perfect. I will let Nathan know we are leaving soon."

I get off the phone and walk to Josh's bedroom. He is lying on his bed, looking at his phone. "Hey, honey, Nathan is gonna come over for a bit, sound good?"

He looks up from the phone screen. "Sure."

"I thought having your best friend over might help."

"That's cool. Of course Nathan can come over."

Fifteen minutes later, Susannah's car pulls up the driveway, and I sling my purse over my shoulder.

Emily finds me in the hallway. "Where are you going?" she asks.

"I'm going to go out with Susannah to bring some food to Lisa. I need to breathe. How are you holding up, honey?"

"I'm all right," she says. "As all right as any of us can be right now."

"I love you," I tell her. "What are you doing now?"

"I love you more, Mom. I'm going to go over to Grandma's. She's making some food for dinner for anyone who's here helping."

"Oh, that is good of her," I say, giving her a quick hug goodbye.

I get into Susannah's car and immediately smell the delicious food she prepared for our friend.

"Enchiladas?" I ask, raising an eyebrow.

"Wow, I'm impressed you could guess."

I give her a smile despite everything. "Well, it's your signature dish."

She grins. "It is. Sorry, I feel bad. I shouldn't be smiling at a time like this. I'm sorry," she says.

"It's all right," I say, buckling up.

She reverses her car and we get on the main road, headed toward Lisa's place. "The timing of this is brutal," she says.

"I know. Out of all the times your daughter could be kidnapped, does it have to be the same weekend that one of your best friends' daughter is found dead?" I shake my head, not understanding why the world feels so cruel.

"It's literally the plot of a book or something, a Netflix documentary," she says.

"Oh, gosh," I say. "I hope not. I don't want to be true crime anything. I want this nightmare to be over, now."

I tell her the information I found on the computer last night as we drive. "Isn't that strange?" I finish.

"It is really strange, Annie," she says slowly, as if really considering her words. "What are you getting at, in pointing out the connection between the places your husband worked and these girls were taken?"

"I don't know," I say. "It just feels weird, not to mention it."

"You don't think there's anything to it?"

"Anything to what? Do I think David is a killer? No, of course not."

"Well, good, because, if there was even the slightest sense that he could be, you've really omitted a lot of details about your marriage over the years."

I exhale, unrolling the window. The weather is mild, and I'm grateful for that. If it were raining or storming, it would be hard for the search. "David and I have a good marriage," I tell her. "We always have. He works a lot, but I have Sarah around to help me."

"I'm glad I don't have my in-laws anywhere near me," Susannah says with a chuckle. "Terry's parents are so overbearing."

I smirk. "Nothing like Terry, then, huh?" I ask, thinking of her easy-going husband.

"He is the odd man out of that bunch, for sure." She sighs. "But honestly, are they making any headway at all on the case? Any leads with Jubilee?"

I tell her about the surveillance cameras. "And," I add, "they're going to look into her foster family, see if they've heard anything from her. I mean, maybe Jubilee called them from a pay phone or something."

"I don't know. Are there even pay phones anywhere, anymore?"

I frown. "Actually, you're right. I don't think there's a pay phone anywhere, but she could have asked to borrow someone's phone and placed a call? Maybe the foster family has heard something."

"When did you give the detective that idea?"

"Around eight o'clock this morning."

"It's afternoon. I think if there were something to go off of with that, you'd have known by now."

"You're probably right," I say. I pull open my phone, hoping against hope that I have a missed call from David or Detective Montgomery, with a new update. Nothing from them, but I have more texts from thoughtful friends from the church.

"Is it overwhelming?" she asks, glancing over at my phone in my hand. "All the people offering support?"

"It is," I tell her. "But I can only imagine what Lisa's going through. It must be so much more to take in."

"I don't know. I think everyone expected Leah to be gone. To be found dead, if found at all. It's been six months."

"How did she do it?" I ask, "How did Lisa survive for six months not having closure? I'm feeling insane after twenty-four hours."

"Don't," she says, reaching over and grasping my hand. "Don't go down that rabbit trail. Not now, not yet. It's too early. There's still hope. Plenty of reasons to have hope. You'll find Jubilee. It's not over."

We pull up to Lisa's house and get out of the car. Susannah reaches for the casserole dish in the backseat, and together, we walk up the main steps to Lisa's door. One of her daughters welcomes us into the house, and we slip off our shoes before following the sound of Lisa's voice in the kitchen, in the back of the house.

"Hey," Susannah says, upon seeing Lisa.

Lisa's face falls. "Oh, you didn't have to do this."

"Of course I did," Susannah says. "I wish it was more than dinner. Terry mentioned coming by this weekend and mowing the lawn, or whatever else you might need done around here."

Lisa's eyes filled with tears. She immediately begins blinking them away. I see the tissue box on the hutch and hand it to her. "You are all so good to us."

"Here," I say. "You can cry freely. You don't have to fight those tears anymore."

She pulls out a tissue and dabs her eye. "How are you holding up?" she asks, putting the focus back on me.

I shrug, "Terribly. Heartbreakingly. Like anything could knock me over, and I might never recover."

Lisa swallows. "Doesn't it feel like just yesterday we were doing all of this for Leah? The search, the detectives, the news reports? And now we're doing it again, but for Jubilee. It doesn't seem right, does it?"

I shake my head. It doesn't. Everything about this feels wrong. "So, the memorial service," I say, trying to switch the subject. "It's in two days?"

She wipes her eyes and nods. "Yeah, my in-laws and parents are going to be able to make it by then. They're getting on a flight today. The memorial itself will be held at the church, of course, and there'll be a graveside service as well. I picked out the casket this morning." Lisa starts to sob, her shoulders shaking, and Susannah and I step close to her, wrapping our arms around her.

I look over Lisa's shoulder and see her younger kids watching us through the doorway, tears in everyone's eyes. This whole house so full of people, so many young children, and yet, so much heartbreak.

I hope Jubilee wasn't taken. I hope she was just a little girl who was playing hide and go seek.

It can't be more than that. If what happened to her is the same thing that happened to Leah, I wouldn't wish this on anyone. This is a living hell.

I press my lips together, hating the pain she's in, and terrified to my core that I'll be living in this same hell soon enough.

CHAPTER 26

Leah
One month earlier

One thing about the people who have kidnapped us is, they are not as close-minded as my parents are.

In my family, I wasn't allowed to check out books from the library without parental approval. There were certain authors that were banned and certain stories that were not allowed, and Mom always read the back covers before we began any book. We had our own bookshelf in the house, filled with novels that she deemed appropriate.

Here, though, we have a lot more leeway. While Carrie and Lindy sit for hours at the kitchen table, putting together puzzles with a thousand pieces, I read. I've read more in the last five months than I've ever read in my entire life. I'm learning a lot about the human condition. About love, about death, about the great beyond.

I had always seen the world in black and white, a set of rules, Heaven and Hell and asking forgiveness whenever you made a mistake. But I read books now like *The Brothers Karamazov*, *Wuthering Heights*, and *Catcher in the Rye* and suddenly I'm seeing everything differently. Brighter, more vivid

— which is an ironic contrast when you think about it, because I'm locked up here, trapped in this dollhouse while my mind has been exploring territory I've never even considered before. It's a cruel joke.

But no matter how many times I ask for a new book, writing a request on the notepad stuck to the fridge, I'm awarded one. Most of the time they're used copies. But sometimes they're new. It doesn't matter to me if they're already dog-eared or if their spines are cracked. When I read a particularly good one, one that I know the other girls will enjoy, I hand it over, telling them they've got to read it, because I want to talk about these stories with someone. Anyone.

But deep down, I really want to talk about these stories with Josh.

I miss him so much.

When I get out of here, I wonder if Josh and I could have a future, now that my life has gone so differently than his.

Five months can change someone quite a bit. I think I used to be more optimistic, more understanding, more gracious, more accommodating. But now that I've been stuck here, having zero control, I realize how much I'd like to change about my life.

I'd like control over what I read, sure, but also what I wear and what I think and where I go. My parents are good parents. My mom has always done her best to take care of us, and she stayed at home so that we could have a very safe and secure life. My dad, he works hard too. He's been a mechanic for two decades. He works with his hands, and his back is always hurting, but he does what he can to make sure he can take care of all of us kids.

They're good to me — strict, sure, but they've never hurt me, not in a way that these people are hurting me now. Yet how could I go back to that kind of shelter? To that kind of life, where I go to church and co-op and stay at home and cook food and take care of my younger siblings?

I don't want to be trapped, in any sense of the word. I want to be set free.

Some of it seems so silly, because I read a book like *War and Peace* and suddenly life is so much bigger. The lens is zoomed out, and I see the world differently. I see *me* differently. What if I went to new places? What if I learned new things? What if I walked the streets of New York City and smoked a cigarette and took a class at a college? What if I got out of the box altogether, and not just this one in the basement? I mean, the *entirety* of the life I've known.

I'm lying on the couch with a copy of *Pride and Prejudice* against my chest.

I'm holding the book with both hands as if it's something holy, as if it's something precious, and maybe it is because I heard once that words are spells. That's where "spelling" comes from. And so maybe all of this, these stories I read, are incantations. Some sort of magic meant just for me. My way out of here.

"What are you doing?" Tamara asks. "Just lying there like that, like a zombie?"

I don't have the energy to sit up. "I was just thinking," I say.

"What are you thinking about?" Tamara asks.

She lifts up my feet, setting them back down on her lap as she flops onto the couch. She looks over at me. After five months, we've become so familiar. The curve of her nose, the way her freckles form constellations on her arms, the sheen of her face, always a little bit oily.

"I was thinking about how one time I fell in love," I tell her. Darcy and Elizabeth, their ardent confessions.

"You fell in love before?" she asks. Her eyes bore into mine. "What do you mean?"

I shrug, sighing, adjusting the pillow underneath my head, staring up at the ceiling. I've kept my cards close since I've moved down here. But maybe it's time I lay everything on the table.

"There was a boy I love. His name's Josh. I've known him since I was a little kid."

"Did he love you?"

"Yeah," I tell her. "He told me he loved me on my birthday. That was the night I was taken."

I look over at Tamara now, wanting to gauge her reaction. She was taken when she was ten, so she missed out on any magic like that, on those sorts of word spells. Hexes like *I love you.*

"I wonder if I'll ever be in love," Tamara says.

"Of course you will," I say. "You're only nineteen. There's plenty of time for love in your lifetime."

"You think?" she says.

Now she's looking at me, but *really* looking at me, like thinking about things.

"Here," I say. "Read *Pride and Prejudice.*" I hand her the copy. "You're going to devour it. It's all about love."

She twists her lip but takes the copy. "I don't know the last time I finished a book."

"Why don't you ever read?" I ask.

"You want to know the truth?"

"Of course," I say. "That's why I asked it."

"I don't like reading like you do, because it makes me sad. I feel like I'm going to be here forever."

Her words are so soft now, a whisper, and I know she's scared of Mother and Father, that the people who keep us trapped down here, will hear. Her voice cracks under the weight of her truth.

It breaks my heart to think about never having love again, having a life, never seeing a baby again, never going to new cities. My family.

Tears fill her eyes. She tries to give me the book back. "I don't want it."

"Read it," I say.

"Why? It'll just make me more sad."

I shake my head ever so slightly and I reach for her hand, turning it over, and in her palm, I trace an H, an O, a P and an E.

I may not be able to say it out loud, and I may not know how it's going to happen exactly, but still I have hope for us yet.

I have hope for all of us trapped down here.

CHAPTER 27

Annie

When I get home from Lisa's, my whole body feels the exhaustion of the last few days. I slept so poorly last night, tossing and turning until I got up and started reading articles in the newspaper, and now that lack of sleep is catching up with me, plus this pounding headache.

Every thought seems to create more tension between my temples; I feel like I could burst. I hate feeling like this, like everything has suddenly gotten completely out of control. Feeling like suddenly my life no longer makes sense.

I crawl into bed next to David, and he wraps an arm around me. I snuggle close against his chest and close my eyes.

"How was everything at Lisa's?" he asks.

"Terrible," I admit, my voice soft.

"It's horrible," David says. "Everything about this. Leah and Jubilee."

"I know," I say, running my hand over his bare chest. "It's hard to believe this is actually my life, our life. She's missing, David. She's really gone." Tears well up in my eyes.

"Shh, shh, it's okay, baby," he tells me. But my shoulders begin to shake and I sob against my husband's chest. A man I've known for more than half my life, who's been my rock, my saving grace, my whole wide world.

"I'm scared," I tell him. "She's just a little girl. She's somewhere all alone."

"I know. I know. But everyone's working hard. They're going to find her."

"They never found Leah," I say, the tears falling freely, my voice parched with emotion, raw and ragged.

"I know, but," he says, "there's no easy answer. There's nothing I can say that's going to make this better. The only thing that's going to make this better is Jubilee being home. So we're going to wake up tomorrow and we're going to try again. All right? That's all we can do right now, sweetie."

I gulp, wiping my eyes. "I know," I say, rolling away from him. My head on my pillow, my eyes at the dark sky, the dark ceiling above. "I have such a bad headache."

"Maybe a good cry will help."

"Maybe." I place my hand over my eyes, my lips still trembling, my heart pounding and then breaking.

"Come here," he says, pulling me toward him. I roll against my husband and wrap my arms around his neck. He kisses me softly and maybe it's wrong to make love at a moment like this, when our world is unraveling, but maybe it's just right, to move against the man who knows me better than anyone else.

"I love you," he tells me, as he takes me to the edge.

I exhale, finding the release I need as the tears stream down my cheeks and he holds me close to him. Our bodies one, and our hearts linked. "We'll get through this, right?" I ask, in a whisper.

He runs his hand over my cheek, tucking my hair behind my ear. "We've gotten through other things. We'll get through this, too. We'll find our girl. She'll come back home. It's all going to be fine."

I cling to him all night long. I sleep soundly against him. And in the morning, I wake to the headache gone. My eyes puffy and red, but I don't care. There may be a ball in the pit of my stomach, but I also have a renewed sense of resolve, a feeling like today is the day we find Jubilee. We can't let another twenty-four hours pass without our little girl back home.

I dress quickly, and when I walk into the kitchen, I thank Emily for making a pot of coffee.

"Mom, of course," she says. "I'll do anything I can to help. I know it's all so much."

"Are the police crews here?" I ask, looking around the kitchen and out the back window over the sink.

Josh enters the kitchen. "Hey, Mom," he says, "Detective Montgomery's here. He's with Dad."

I take my cup of coffee, squeezing his shoulder before walking into the living room. David is there, talking to the detective. "Is there an update?" I ask.

"Unfortunately," Montgomery begins, "not much to report. I did want you to know, though, that we contacted the foster family. They have had no word from Jubilee. I know that doesn't make it better or worse. At least that road is closed for now. Of course, we'll hear more if something crops up. They were very willing to answer our questions and wanted to send all of their love to your whole family and want you to know they're praying for you."

I reach out for David's hand and squeeze it. "Thank you, detective," I say. "I can't imagine her traveling that far, but I suppose anything's possible right now."

Montgomery nods. "Unfortunately, yes, that's the truth. We're well past forty-eight hours with her as a missing person, and—"

"I know," David says, cutting him off. "I've read the statistics."

"What are the statistics?" I ask my husband.

He clenches his jaw. "Annie," he says softly, "it's not good."

"But last night," I began swallowing, "you promised, you said everything was going to be okay."

He wraps an arm around me, and I watch as he meets the detective's gaze. I stop talking, because I realize how

135

ridiculous I sound. Promises made in the middle of the night don't mean that my daughter is coming home anytime soon.

The detective leaves, and I ask David what he's up to. "I have to do a little bit of work, go on site. The build out in Belvedere is getting wrapped up, but I need to go through a few checklists. My dad's going to come out with me."

"That makes sense," I say. "Do you need me to pack you some food? Coffee to go?"

"I already had a cup," he says, "and I ate. Emily's a champ; she made banana bread. I don't know when she had the energy to do that."

I sigh. "She's probably not sleeping, either."

David cups my cheek. "You slept pretty good last night."

I close my eyes, remembering. "Thankfully," I say. "I love you, David."

"I love you more, Annie. I promise it's going to be okay. I'm just going to be gone for a few hours. All right?"

"Okay." He leaves, and my house suddenly feels so quiet. Even though the boys are here, and Emily, it's different without my husband at my side. With him, I feel like I have an extra sense of strength.

Maybe I need to gather my own strength right now. Maybe that's what Jubilee needs.

My phone rings and I answer it, seeing that it's Elijah. I know his dad's been keeping him up to date on everything that's been going on here. "Hey, Mom," he says, "I know you are scared, but I just want you to know I love you."

"Thank you," I say, "I love you, too."

"I've never even met her, you know?" Elijah says, "But I know how much you love her, Mom. She'll come home."

"I hope so," I say.

"I know so," he tells me. "Look, I have to go on base, but I just wanted to call quick to let you know I love you and am thinking about you."

"Thank you, honey. That means more than you know. And if you get a chance, will you call Josh?" I ask him. "He's actually been having a really hard time. Dad told you about Leah?"

"Yes," Elijah says, "he did. The service is tomorrow?"

"Yeah," I tell him. "It's going to be a hard day. Harder than ever, considering that Jubilee's not here."

"She'll be back by then," Elijah tells me. "I know it."

I end the call thanking God for a son like that. For someone who calls to check on me to make sure I'm okay.

I slide my phone in my back jeans pocket, and then the doorbell rings. I walk to answer it and am greeted by someone I've never seen before.

"Hello?" It's a young man says in his mid-thirties. He's wearing a suit, dark navy, with a slender tie. "I'm Tom Claymore."

"Do I know you?" I ask, already knowing I don't.

"I'm a writer for the *Seattle Sun*."

"Right," I say. "I'm not answering any questions. Thank you, though."

"There is an Amber alert and Detective Montgomery, with the State Police, is working on the case."

"Those things are true, but like I said," I tell him, "I'm really not in a place to do this. It's been a long few days, and—"

"I know, but listen. I want to talk to you about some things I've uncovered, things you might not know."

I shake my head, shutting my front door and stepping onto the porch, not wanting the boys inside to hear any of this. "Look," I say, "I don't want to talk to you about anything to do with my daughter."

"This doesn't have anything to do with your daughter. This has to do with your husband, David."

I swallow. "You're here to talk to David?"

"No, not talk to David, talk to you."

"I don't understand," I say. "I'm just trying to keep things together right now. My daughter's been missing, and . . ."

"I know, and I'm so sorry. I heard about your daughter on the news, and of course, I've been following it closely with the police blotters, but I began looking into other missing girls here."

"What do you mean?" I ask, playing dumb.

"The missing girls in this county over the last ten years. It is all very interesting."

"What's interesting?" I ask.

"Well, I cross-referenced your husband's name, knowing the line of work he does."

"Why would you even do that?" I ask.

Claymore shrugs. "A sixth sense. Something seemed off, odd. I knew he was a contractor in the county and with a few searches of public records, I saw what permits he'd gotten and when. It clicked when I saw a few of the dates and a few of the names coincide."

"What are you trying to insinuate?" I ask.

"Nothing. Nothing," he says, lifting his hands. "Look, I'm not trying to start anything."

"Except you came to my house, to my porch, and started accusing my husband of something heinous. That's not nothing. That's horrific," I say. "My husband and his company have been a longstanding pillar in this community. They're upright. They are good men, and it is an ethical and morally sound business. How dare you come here and say anything otherwise?"

"Yeah," Claymore says, "I get it. I get it. I'm not trying to fight with you. I just thought you might like to know, so you could go do some sleuthing on your own."

"I already know what you're talking about."

His eyebrows raise. "Oh yeah? So you were putting pieces together, too."

"There's nothing to piece together."

Claymore shrugs. "Maybe, but you know how Ted Bundy manned a rape hotline?"

My blood begins to curdle. I want to spit something. I want to say something vile. "How dare you?" I say. "You need to leave now."

"Fine," he says, "but listen, if you change your mind—"

"I won't," I say. I turn around, pushing open my front door and slamming it without another glance back.

CHAPTER 28

Jubilee
One week earlier

Mom is running the boys into town for some new clothes, blue jeans, and tennis shoes. Lucky for me, I get to hang out with Grandma Sarah in her kitchen.

Grandma looks at me with a smile. She's wearing an apron and has two smaller aprons in her hand. "Which one do you want to wear?" she asks. Her face is bright. Her cheeks are always pink and rosy, and her long gray hair is in a braid. "Do you want to wear pink or purple?"

"Purple," I say, with a smile, and she tosses it to me with a laugh. I pull it on over my head, and she walks up to me, tying the back into a bow.

"Perfect. Now, next question," she asks. "Would you like to make peach cobbler or banana bread?"

I press my lips together, trying to decide. "Hmm, peach cobbler," I say.

"You're a big peach fan?" Grandma asks.

I shake my head. "No, I just don't think I've ever had it."

"Ah," she says. "Well, then, this is the perfect time for us to make it. Come on over here. I got a stool for you." I follow her around to the pantry, and she pulls open the big wooden doors. "Can you get me the flour?" she asks.

I look over at her, thinking she was going to do this part, but it's fun, her letting me be the grownup. I reach for a bin that says flour and hand it to her.

"Perfect." She takes it from me and sets it on the kitchen counter. "Now, we need sugar. White sugar."

I run my eyes over the shelf of dry goods, identifying the bin of sugar. "This one?"

She nods. "That's the one."

I hand it to her and she continues the list of ingredients. It's like she knows everything she needs for the recipe just in her head. That's one good thing I've learned about grandmas. They're smart like that. At least this one is. She knows things without looking it up. I get out the baking soda and the vanilla. In the fridge, I take out butter and milk and an egg.

I look around the kitchen counter. "Where's the peaches?"

"Those are in the pantry," she says. "Not this pantry. The big one, in the basement."

"I've never been down there," I tell her.

"Huh? Home almost three months and you've never been to Grandma's pantry? Well, let's change that right now," she says. "Come on."

We walk down the hall and there's a door. She tells me to open it and she flips on a light.

"It looks creepy," I say.

"It's not," she says. "I promise. Your grandpa is really handy, and he's fixed most of this up for me. Look, the walls are painted. There's even carpet on the stairs."

We go down to the pantry, and my eyes widen. "Oh my goodness," I say, taking it all in. "And I thought Mom had a lot of food stocked up in case of an emergency."

Grandma laughs. "This is what I do in the summer. And this summer you're going to be my sous-chef. Well, my partner in crime."

We walk in her pantry, and I see rows and rows of clear jars filled with the garden. "Pickles," Grandma says, "green beans, jellies, all sorts. Strawberry, grape, blackberry, raspberry."

"What are these?" I ask, pulling a jar from the shelf.

"Those are the sauces. Hot sauce, salsa verde, enchilada sauce, and spaghetti sauce. That's from the tomato garden," she says, with a smile, "and over here is all the fruit."

"That's a lot of fruit," I say. "Applesauce?"

"Yep," she says. "Some with cinnamon," and then she points to another row, "some without. We have pears and cherries . . . and look, we have the peaches over here."

"They look so pretty."

"Right?" she says. "Well, I don't get all the peaches from the two peach trees that we have on this property. I always have your grandpa go over the mountains for me during peach season and get pallets of them."

"What's over the mountains?" I ask.

"Well, that's where there's lots of farms. So, he can buy them in big boxes for me, and then he brings them home and I get to work. I spend a week just canning up all these peaches, and I spend the rest of the year eating them and sharing them. Your mom's best friend, Susannah, she likes to can, too. Sometimes she'll come over here in the summer and we'll get a bunch done together."

"Except this summer," I say, "I'll be there too, right?"

"Exactly. You like pickles?"

I nod. "Yeah, I think so."

"Well, I make the best bread-and-butter pickles in the whole wide world."

I giggle. "Did you win a contest or something to prove that?"

"As a matter of fact, I did," Grandma says. She takes two jars of the peaches off the shelf. "At the county fair. Now, that's another thing we'll have to do together. Go to the fair. But that's not until the fall. The end of harvest."

I smile at her, trying to understand what she's talking about. So many new words she says at rapid speed, canning and ribbons and fairs. But I can picture it, being in the garden with her and picking these green beans, and bringing them in the house and somehow making something happen with them to bring them down to the pantry.

"All right," she says, "let's go back up."

"What's back there? Is it another cellar?" I ask, pointing to a small, narrow door at the end of the row of canned goods.

"Oh, this is an old house, and that's an old door that used to lead to the barn a hundred years ago. But it's off-limits, all right? Grandpa says it's not safe."

"All right," I say. "Is it dangerous?"

"Maybe," she says, turning with a smile. "I think it must just have some creepy crawly bugs, though!"

I giggle. "Bugs don't scare me." I follow Grandma back upstairs, to the kitchen.

We make the cobbler. We put the sliced peaches at the bottom of a pan and put the batter we prepare on top of it. "Then you sprinkle the sugar on top of the batter," she says, "spread evenly."

"Okay," I say, smiling.

"And then here, take this. Half a cup of hot water and pour it over the sugar so when it bakes, it gives it an extra crunchy crust."

We slide it into the oven and set a timer. She flips on the oven light so I can watch it bubble up. While it's cooking, she makes us tea. English breakfast, her favorite. She puts sugar and milk in both of ours, and we sit at the kitchen table, waiting for the cobbler.

She shows me her notepad. "What's this?" I ask.

"Well, this is everything that I'm going to put in the garden this spring. It's almost time to plant."

"You do this every year? Make a drawing of your garden?"

She smiles. "Yep. I like to make notes, so everything's planted in just the right place."

I smile at her — beaming, really. "You're my first grandma," I tell her. "The first grandma I ever had."

The oven timer goes off, and I think she's going to jump up and get the cobbler, but instead, she takes my hand and she smiles. "And you're my youngest granddaughter. The youngest granddaughter I've ever had."

She scrunches up her nose and I scrunch mine up back. And I feel this warmth in my belly, in my heart, in my whole body. And it has nothing to do with the cobbler. It has everything to do with this moment, with having a grandma for the first time. With being hers.

CHAPTER 29

Annie

My blood boils as I walk back into the house. I don't know what that reporter was thinking, but he's disgusting.

"Who was that?" Josh and Andrew ask when I enter the kitchen.

"It doesn't matter," I say.

"Mom, who was that guy out there?"

"A reporter," I say, pressing my fingers into my temples, the headache returning.

"A reporter from where?"

"The *Seattle Sun*," I say.

"Do you want me to call Dad?" Andrew asks.

I shake my head. "He went to his job site. He's got to do work. We can't just stop everything, even though it's all I want to do."

"Mom," Andrew says, taking me by the shoulders. "Calm down."

It's only then I realize I'm hyperventilating, my hands bracing against the countertop as I breathe in and out deeply, staggering. "Oh my God," I say, "the things he was saying.

He thinks your dad had something to do with it. I don't understand."

"Dad?" Emily says. "What do you mean? Do with what?"

"It doesn't matter," I say.

"Is this about what you were reading the other night on the computer?"

"You saw that?" I ask Josh.

"Of course I saw it. You had a ton of articles pulled up on the computer."

"God," I say. "I was hoping you hadn't seen."

"What kind of articles?" Andrew asks.

Josh fills him in. "A bunch of girls have gone missing over the years, just like Leah, and weirdly, they were in the same counties that dad was in when he was working on his builds."

"What are you trying to say?" Andrew says.

Josh lifts his hands in defense. "I'm not saying anything. It was Mom who was looking."

"I'm not saying anything, either," I say. "It was the reporter who was asking."

"Who is that man?" Andrew asks. "What was his name? Claymore? Clayborn?"

"I'm not sure," I say.

"Did he give you a card?"

"He tried to," I say. "I didn't want anything from him. I'm not going to talk to him again. The things he was insinuating about your dad, it's horrible."

Emily presses her lips together. "Mom, I don't understand what you're talking about. Not exactly. I haven't read any articles, and I don't know who this reporter is, but if someone thinks Dad did something bad to Jubilee or Leah or anyone, you have to help prove him wrong. You can't have a reporter write stories about Dad like that."

Just then, there's another knock on the door. "Are you kidding me?" I ask. "What else?"

But this time it's Detective Montgomery, with two state officers. "What is it now?" I ask. My whole morning has been a disaster, confusing.

"We need to go through David's office."

"You can't just search his office," I say.

"Actually," Detective Montgomery says, "we have a warrant to do so."

I shake my head. "That's not possible. You went and got a warrant against David, right now, when we're looking for Jubilee? What is this about?"

"We need to go through his records, Annie," Montgomery tells me.

I frown. "Is this about what that reporter was saying about the missing girls?"

Montgomery looks at me, a hard look, a look he's never given me before. A look that says, *Annie, you are so out of your depths. Tread carefully.*

But I'm not going to sink. I was made to swim.

"I don't know what you have the right to look at," I say, "but if you have the warrant, his office is at the end of the hall. He has a desk in there. It's where he keeps everything."

"We're doing this to clear his name," Montgomery says. "I don't think your husband has done anything, but there are allegations, and it's our job to see them through."

"Fine," I say. "Do what you have to. I mean, I suppose the reporters are going to dig through our life soon enough. If a story like this is breaking, that David may have had something to do with his daughter being kidnapped, and the other girls and Leah, and . . ."

Montgomery lifts a hand. "Listen," he says. "I'm not here to rile you up and start a fight. I'm here with the facts, and the facts are, we need to go through the records."

"Fine," I say. "Andrew, can you help?"

He nods, ushering the officers down the hall.

I pull out my phone. "David?" I say, when he picks up.

"What is it, Annie?"

"It's bad." I tell him that the officers are here and what they're here for.

"Don't worry about it," he says calmly. "They're doing their due diligence. That's a good thing. We want to have officers on the case who aren't cutting any corners. That's how we're going to find Jubilee."

"We're not going to find Jubilee if they're spending their time looking in your record books," I say.

There's a pause. "We don't know anything about due process, but I do know that we have to trust these men to do their job to find our daughter."

"Fine," I say, "but you know that's not very comforting."

"I'm sorry, Annie. I wish I was there. I'm sorry that the officers came when you were alone."

"I'm not alone. The boys are here. Emily, too."

"Do you want my mom to come over?"

"No," I say. "It's fine. It's just been a lot. There was a reporter here."

"Tom Claymore?"

"You know him?" I ask.

"He called me earlier. I told him I wasn't available. I guess he didn't like that. He came to the house?"

"Yes," I say, "he did. But the things he was saying, David, it's not good."

"Hey, it's going to be all right. We're going to get through this. Like I told you this morning, like I told you last night, we can get through anything, Annie."

I exhale. "I hope you're right."

I end the phone call and walk down the hall toward my husband's office. I listen outside the doorway to what the officers are saying. I hear one of them speak. *"It looks like he was using day workers for years, which means most of these people are going to be impossible to trace."*

"I know it's early to say, but there's no way it was David. At least, I don't think so. The man is a stand-up guy," Montgomery says. "But someone on his crew, who's been on his crew for a long time, may have had something to do with this."

I walk away, not wanting to hear any more, not wanting to think what this could mean for David's business. It's how our entire family is supported. My in-laws, too. If someone connected to this construction company has been kidnapping and murdering girls for years . . .

I swallow, the headache pounding. My phone rings. It's Susannah.

"What is it?" I ask.

"Have you read the news?"

She texts me the article from the *Seattle Sun*, which has just been posted, and I realize Tom Claymore must have been planning on writing it before he even came to my house.

This article lays out the basic facts; I'm guessing he was coming to me to get a follow-up. It's everything I already know, the facts of my daughter's kidnapping laid out. It identifies the detective in charge, and there are members of the community interviewed.

"We haven't known Jubilee long, but she is a lovely young girl. We just want her home safe with her family." It's a quote by Marsha Callahan, a member of our church. I appreciate her kindness but hate the idea of a reporter coming to her and asking questions. It's not fair. The level of intrusiveness feels dirty. Something I don't want any part of.

I swallow, reading on, and see that Claymore has connected the other murders and missing girls with Jubilee. I know he is a reporter, and it's his job to write this story, but he doesn't have all the facts.

Yes, there have been girls who have gone missing in this county, and yes, Jubilee going missing right after Leah's body was found dead feels suspect. But none of the other girls were taken in such close proximity to one another, and Jubilee is younger.

"This is ridiculous," I mutter under my breath.

Mason comes up behind me. "What is it, Mom?"

I hand him my phone, and he reads.

"Oh. Gosh, is this really what people think?" he asks. "What people are saying that Jubilee was a victim of?"

I blink back the tears. "I don't know what to think, but it doesn't sound good, does it?"

"It doesn't, Mom," he says, handing me back the phone. "That was the reporter who was here earlier?"

I nod. "Yeah, I guess they'd called Dad and asked him questions, too. Probably wanting a follow-up article to this."

"It doesn't have to mean anything," Mason says. He's my youngest boy, and somehow he feels so wise in this moment. "Just forget about it, Mom. Just have faith in Jubilee and the detectives. We're going to find her."

"I hope you're right," I say. He gives me a hug, and it's one of those hugs that as a mother you hold onto, tight, that you savor, that you don't let go of too quickly. I've raised enough boys to know that hugs like this are fleeting, and that soon he won't be a "young man." He will be a man in his own right, and he won't hug me in this tender way anymore. He won't be my little goose. He will be grown.

"I love you so much," I say.

"I love you more, Mom," he tells me, and I believe him. I know he loves me with all his heart.

"I just wish we'd had more time with Jubilee before she left . . . before she was taken. She's so young."

"I know," he says, "I know."

Detective Montgomery and the officers walk down the hall and find me in the living room with Mason.

"Did you get everything you were looking for?" I ask. They nod. They're holding some boxes, items they must be confiscating. "If you need anything else, let me know. I can help. I . . ." But my voice breaks, and tears spill from my eyes. I just want this nightmare to end.

Montgomery nods. "I appreciate it, but at the moment we're going to focus on finding Jubilee, and you are going to focus on thinking of places she may have gone. What were her favorite restaurants in town, her favorite stores, and what did she like to do for fun? The more you can think about that and give us ideas of where to look and where the search can go, the better."

"Right," I say.

Mason perks up. "Her and I, when we weren't playing in the woods, sometimes we'd ride a bike down to Gilmore Pond."

Detective Montgomery frowns. "No one's mentioned that."

Mason looks distraught. "Sorry, I didn't realize I was supposed to. I've been out on the search too, but it's about a two-mile bike ride. It's not far. We go there sometimes, and I just throw rocks in the water, and we planned on going fishing this summer. There's trout down there, and I told her how last year I caught three. She thought that sounded fun because she'd never gone fishing before."

I look at Mason, appreciating his offer of information. "Maybe she's there," I say. "Has anyone looked at the pond?"

"We'll have to add it to our search grid," Montgomery says, "but I appreciate it. This is helpful. That's the kind of thing we need right now. We don't know Jubilee like you do. We don't know her at all, so anything you can do to help us will mean everything for the case." Montgomery leaves with the officers, and Mason tells me he's going to go walk the yard again.

"What for?" I ask.

"Just in case we missed anything. Josh and I were going to head out."

"Okay, honey, I love you."

"I love you more." He walks away, and I head down the hall to David's office. I know Montgomery just rifled through everything in here, but I'm curious to see what's been left behind. If there's any duplicates that could give me information.

It looks like they've taken his laptop computer and his files, but they haven't taken the photographs that are lining the wall, pictures of our family over the years. I was the one who framed them and hung them to make a gallery. And there are some pictures of office or crew barbecues that we hold every summer.

I look at the last few ones, smiling at familiar faces, frowning when I realize it's not only day workers whom he has employed. There are some guys who have been working for a handful of years for David, but as I scan the photos, I realize there's one person who's been working for David for decades. Robert Pascal.

He's always worked here, never been married. He lives in town in a trailer. He's a hard worker, a man in his forties. I don't really know anything about him, just that he's quiet and keeps to himself. He doesn't come to church except for Christmas and Easter. I wonder about him, though, because as I look through the photographs hanging on the wall, I realize he's been at every single barbecue we've ever held. He's a nice guy. He's always friendly, plays catch with the kids and helps flip burgers when he comes once a year to the backyard.

I bite my bottom lip, wondering about him, and I pull out my phone, typing his name into the internet search engine: Robert Pascal of Thomas County.

I swallow as a few results pull up. My heart pounds as I click past his Facebook profile and click around. Nothing. Not knowing anything about him puts me at a disadvantage. But I am also only really interested in a potential criminal background. That is what will give me something to go off of. I type in his name and add Washington state public records. There is a charge from eleven years ago.

I click on it and begin to read. He has been charged with interference of child custody. I swallow, wanting to understand.

According to the report, Robert Pascal was charged with parental interference, meaning he deprived the mother of her child visitation or custody time.

I quickly google the words parental interference. This explains that an offending parent may hide children, refuse to return them or remove them from the state without permission.

Hide children?

My heart falls.

David couldn't have known this. He wouldn't have knowingly hired a man who made life hellish for the mother of his child, would he?

I didn't even know Robert was a father.

No, I think. It's not possible. I close the phone, not wanting to read anymore, not wanting to think that any of this could be true.

It makes me sick, as I look back at the photograph on the wall in the husband's office.

Could it be?

I need a distraction. In the kitchen, I begin preparing meals for the rest of the day, focusing on what I can control.

I don't know who will be here at the house this evening, but anyone who is around will need to eat. I make a big batch of my famous macaroni and cheese, sliding it into the oven, and then I make chicken salad with cans of chicken that are in the pantry. Pulling out a loaf of bread, I assemble a plate full of sandwiches. By the time I'm done, it's four in the afternoon.

The front door opens, it's David. He walks in the kitchen and gives me a hug, kissing my cheek.

"Did you see the paper?" I ask him.

He nods. "Yeah, we all read it on site. It's pretty grim."

"I'm so sorry," I say. "At least it didn't link any of those missing girls to you or the company."

"It's bullshit," he says. "I know I never swear, but my God, Claymore is a real piece of work. It's slander."

"Well, it will be slander if he starts connecting it to your firm."

David sits down at a stool at the island, and I pull out a plate, placing a sandwich on it. "Do you want some chips?" I ask. He nods and I grab him a Coke from the fridge, a bag of potato chips. He begins to eat as I brace myself to ask the questions that scare me.

"The detective was here and took things from your office," I start. "It looks like your laptop and your files, but I have to ask you something, David."

"What?" he asks, taking another bite of the sandwich. I swallow.

"I need to ask you about Robert Pascal. He's worked for you for decades, and I looked him up on the computer."

"And what did you find?" His eyes meet mine. I know he knows.

"How could you have him come here, to our home, where our children are?"

"What do you mean?" David asks, frowning.

"He interfered with a custody agreement. I don't know the specifics, but—"

"Oh," David says, nodding his head. He opens his can of soda. "I know about that."

"What do you know?"

"It was over a decade ago. His ex-wife was unhinged, and he didn't want his daughter around her."

"Unhinged how?"

David shrugs, nonplussed. "I honestly can't remember, but he took their kid to his mom's house in Arizona, which was a big problem because they crossed state lines. He went to jail for it and was fined massively."

"So he can hide children? He has before."

David runs a hand over his jaw. "What are you getting at, Annie?"

My eyes narrow, feeling flustered. "I am getting at the fact this timing doesn't look good. He might have our daughter."

"He doesn't. He's a good guy," he says. "Besides, he served his time. What do you want? For me to tell you every criminal charge any of the day workers I hire have had? Because I could never find anyone to do work if we went down that road. I'm sure more than half the guys on my crew at any given time have been to jail for a DUI."

"That may be so, and I appreciate you giving people work who have a hard time getting it anywhere else, but he's been to our home for years with our kids, with our young children, our daughter, and—"

"Annie, I don't want to argue with you, but do you hear yourself? He's been coming to our house for years and never once has he done something out of line, something questionable. There's never been an incident. He's never gone to jail again. I thought our faith was about forgiving, about letting the past be in the past."

"This feels different," I say. "This feels really different."

"Would it if this hadn't been going on right now with the girls gone missing and with Jubilee, and—"

"But that is what's happening, right now, to us, to our family, David."

"I never hired him in the first place. It was my dad."

"I don't care if it was James and not you. You went along with it."

"He's been one of the constants on our crew for eight years. Give the guy some slack, Annie."

"But he was here, I say, pressing a hand to my chest, "for the search party yesterday, looking for Jubilee. What if he inserted himself into the search party in order to—"

"In order to what?" David says, his voice tense and tight. "What are you insinuating, Annie?"

"I don't know," I say. "What if he intentionally obscured something? What if he, I don't know, covered tracks that may have been left or what if he found something of Jubilee's in the woods and hid it to protect himself? What if he's—"

"Stop," David says, his voice sharp, harsher than he ever is. "Don't talk like this anymore. It's not okay. Robert has done nothing to give us any idea that he has done something to our daughter, to anyone's daughter."

I shake my head, though, angry. "That's not true, though, is it? He did do something to someone's daughter, his own. So don't tell me I'm being naive, and don't tell me I'm thinking the worst of people right now. All I'm doing is fighting for my little girl to come home. It's not about the good things Robert's done, it's about the fact our little girl is missing, and I don't care if Robert's proved himself loyal to you. The fact remains: Jubilee is gone, and someone has taken her."

CHAPTER 30

Leah
One week earlier

Tamara walks up to me and hands me the copy of *Pride and Prejudice*. "I think out of all the passages, my favorite was chapter eighteen." She smiles, handing me the book. "Would you like anything to eat?" she asks. "I was going to make some tea to have with these brownies."

"Sure," I say. "Sounds good."

With the book in hand, I follow her to the kitchen. I flip through the pages to the chapter she mentioned.

"What do you think?" she asks. "Do you like that chapter, too?"

It's only then I realize she has written in the margins of these pages, of this chapter. I pause, her eyes meet mine. "Just give me a second to reread it," I say. "I'm not quite sure I remember this section exactly."

"Of course," she says. "Do you want mint tea or Earl Grey?"

"Mint," I say. "My stomach's been unsettled."

Her eyes find mine again. The smallest of smiles flickers across her face. "Funny," she says. "For the first time in ages, I feel like my stomach is settled."

I know what she means: that she's had a change of heart, that her intuition is leading her somewhere, that she's no longer scared. When I read her handwriting, tight in the margins, I know my assessment is correct.

We can't sleep tonight. Whatever we do, we have to stay awake. I think we should eat but then throw up.

It's a good idea. But where do we throw up undetected from the cameras? I keep reading, seeing that Tamara has answered my question.

Bathroom shower. Camera angle isn't in there.

She's right. It would be disgusting, of course, for all of us to throw up in the shower, but it's our only choice not to ingest the medication.

I want to fall in love like you did, like Elizabeth Bennett did.

I think of my arrowhead, the one I still have tucked against my chest. I can use it as a weapon, but I don't even know if we'll need that, because five girls up against Mother seems like we could do more damage to her than her to us.

It's the gun, of course, that we have to worry about.

The five of us sit for our snack. We drink our tea. We eat our brownies. "Does anyone else want to read the book?" I ask, passing it around the table as we all sit there eating. Usually, after we eat something like this, we fall asleep within the hour, but this isn't usually.

This is the day everything changes.

Carrie's eyes widened as she reads the pages in the book. Lindy bites her bottom lip after her turn. "This is good," she says. "I had no idea this book was so interesting."

Beth grins. "Oh, I love this," she says.

"Me, too," I say. "It's my favorite book ever. You should read the whole thing," I tell the girls.

Tamara agrees. "I don't know why I was so resistant for so long, but I think you have good taste, Leah."

I smile. "I think I'm actually going to take a shower before I take my nap," I say.

Around the table, the girls nod. "That actually sounds like a really good idea," Lindy says. "Why don't we all take showers and wash our hair, and then we can braid it really tight? Remember those braids we were doing a while ago?"

"Oh, I love that idea," Carrie says, playing along. "We can all braid each other's hair. It will look so pretty and perfect."

"All right," I say. "I'll jump in the shower real quick, and then we can have a braid party before we take a rest."

My sisters, all of us trapped, all of us longing for more.

Love has a hold on us in different ways: love for family, for a future, for experiences, for someone to hold our hand and tell us how ardently they want us.

We deserve that.

It's time we were set free.

CHAPTER 31

Annie

Our pastor joins us in the kitchen. I'm standing there with David, Emily and her fiancé, Jaden.

"Pastor Craig," I say. "Thank you for coming."

He walks over and gives me a hug. David, too.

"We'll get through this. We can get through anything," he says and while I believe him, after the day I've had, I feel lost, like hope is elusive. "I can see the worry in your eyes, Annie. But have faith."

"Lisa had faith," I say, "and Leah's gone."

He nods solemnly, because the words I have said make his condolences empty, shallow.

"Don't make my mom cry again," Emily says. "It's all been so much."

Jaden clears his throat. "Is everyone headed out for the search?"

"I think they're getting started in a few minutes."

I pipe up. "I'm just going to grab my coat. I'll meet you outside."

I walk out of the kitchen and head to the bathroom, knowing I need to splash cold water on my face before anything else. I look in the mirror and take a deep breath.

"Keep yourself together, Annie. Now is not the time to fall apart."

And while I know it's true, it's still so hard when it feels like everything is spiraling out of control. I don't want to look at anyone with judgment, especially not my husband, but everything that I learned about Robert Pascal makes me feel apprehensive.

When I get out of the bathroom, I see Lisa waiting for me. "Oh," I say. "I didn't know you were coming."

"I was at my house crying," she says, "like always. The family is in town for the service and it's all set for tomorrow."

I give her a hug. She keeps talking. "But I knew so many people were going to be here looking for Jubilee and it felt wrong to be just sitting there crying when I could be helping."

"You don't need to help right now, though. Maybe you need to grieve."

"Maybe this is the best way to help grieve," she says, shaking your head. "Doing something is better than just sitting and wallowing in my own sadness. I've been doing that for months."

"Did you see the article?" I ask her.

"Of course I did. It's one of the other reasons I came because even though I want to help find Jubilee, Annie, why didn't you tell me about the connections David had with all of the cases of the missing girls?"

I pulled back in surprise. "How did you know about that?"

"Well, I heard about it, is all."

I frown. "From Susannah?"

She nods. I bite my bottom lip, wondering why Susannah would have said something like that. I confided in her; never in my wildest dreams did I think she would gossip about it.

"Look, David had nothing to do with any of this."

Lisa exhales. "I wasn't saying he was. It's just—"

"I know. It's weird. But we need to focus on Jubilee right now, on Leah, and let the police do their job."

She tries again. "You have no other leads, no ideas of who—"

"If I did, do you think I'd be standing here? No," I say. "I feel as lost as anyone. Can we please just focus on the search party?"

"You're right," Lisa says, running a hand through her hair. "I'm sorry. I'm just so upset. We have no answers."

"I know," I tell her, wrapping my arms around her and giving her a hug.

"But I don't have any idea who could have done this," she said.

I press my lips together, knowing that Lisa needs a win just as badly as I do.

"There's one thing that's weird," I say. "I'm not trying to start rumors," I tell her. "But there's one man that's always been on David's crew, Robert Pascal."

Lisa frowns. "I don't know him."

"Right. He's single. No kids living with him, rarely goes to church. But he has a criminal record."

"Are you serious?" Lisa asks.

"Yes, and he's been on the crew for a long time. But before that, he was charged with parental interference. He took his daughter out of the state without informing his ex."

Lisa's eyes widen. "Oh my gosh," she says pressing a hand over her chest. "What do you mean? Robert kidnapped his own child?"

"It seems like it. David says I am jumping to an extreme . . . but the situation we are in is extreme. David and James are always trying to do good and give people second chances, and Robert's never had anything come up in all of the years he's worked for David. But."

"You're mentioning him now," Lisa says.

Our eyes meet.

"I don't want to think the worst about someone. I want to believe. I want . . ."

Lisa, though, has eyes full of anger. Her gentle spirit has been replaced with something I've never seen in her before.

"Did he do this? Did he kidnap and kill my daughter?"

"Lisa, I don't know anything about that. I don't think it's possible. I think—"

"Yet David's crew was at all of the locations where these girls had gone missing. Robert, a man who's been in jail for taking his child out of state, has been at those locations and you don't think there's anything suspicious? Does anybody know anything about where he lives, about his home, about his life? I've never even heard of him before. All that time, my daughter, your little girl, no. This is too much."

Lisa shakes her head, turns to leave, and I follow her.

"Wait," I say.

But she's already walked outside, calling for her husband. But before we run into him, we see Robert Pascal in the driveway talking with David and some other men.

"What is he doing here?" I ask under my breath.

"Who?" Lisa asks, looking back at me.

"Robert. He's here." I exhale. "He was here the other day, too, helping with the search."

"Of course he was," she says, shaking her head, walking right over to the group of men.

I try to get David's attention, but Lisa is on a mission.

"Are you Robert Pascal?" she asks, stepping up to him.

"Yes, I am. Hello. What was your name?"

She scoffs. "I'm Lisa. My daughter was Leah. You may have heard. She recently died. She was fifteen years old. *Fifteen*, and—"

"Oh, my god. I'm so sorry for your loss," he says. "I did hear about that and—"

"I'm sure you did. I'm sure you heard all about it."

Robert looks over at David, confusion written between his brows.

"Don't play stupid. I know what you are. You're a kidnapper."

A soft gasp echoes through the driveway and the yard. The two dozen people who are standing waiting for the search to begin are watching. I close my eyes, shaking my head, wanting this all to stop right now. I don't want a scene. I just want to find Jubilee.

"You killed her, didn't you? My daughter? And you took Jubilee and you—"

"Look, ma'am, I'm sorry for your loss," Robert says. "But I didn't do anything to your daughter or Jubilee. I'm just . . . I'm just doing my best. I'm just a man doing my best. I didn't—"

Lisa is not letting it go. "As soon as the cops pin this on you, you'll never see the light of day."

Robert, though, is backing away. "I'm sorry," he said. "I'm not looking to fight. I'm not looking for anything. I was here to help David and Annie. But I got to go."

"The police know where you live, you know. You can't hide forever," Lisa calls after him.

"Lisa," I say. "Enough."

Her husband has come over, reaching for her hand. "Sweetie," he says. "It's not our job. It's—"

"But do you know what he did? Do you know what he's done?"

Robert is in his truck, peeling away. Lisa's wrapped up in her husband's embrace, and I look over at David, scared, feeling like everything's unraveling. Detective Montgomery walks over.

"Clearly, I missed something," he says, addressing Lisa, David and me. "But I need to be filled in on everything."

"It's just Lisa. She's — it's nothing to do with anything."

"Oh, yes it is," she says, pulling away from her husband and looking at Montgomery. "I'll tell you everything. That man who just left? He is a killer."

CHAPTER 32

Leah
One week earlier

In the bathroom, I undress with my back to the camera, quickly. Folding my clothes on the floor, Josh's arrowhead tucked against the folds of fabric.

With the water turned on, I brace myself for what will come next. What I must do. Wanting it hot, wanting my skin to burn. Hoping that the noise of the water stream washes away the sound of me retching.

I step under the water. I press a finger in my mouth, deep, to my throat. I choke, gagging on the bile, but desperate to rid myself of the brownie that I just ate.

I try again, knowing we cannot die down here.

With my finger down my throat, I force myself to keel over. And when I empty myself of everything in my stomach, I cough, spitting out the vomit. Tears streak my face. It's painful, more painful than I realized it would be, to force myself to do this.

I squeeze my eyes shut, praying I never have to do this again. Praying that for the rest of my life, I'll be free. I'm not sure exactly how I am going to tackle Mother and get out of that apartment, but I sure as hell am going to try.

The other girls need to get in the shower before the laced brownies enter their bloodstream. I turn off the water, filled with resolve.

No more waiting. Now, it's time to live.

CHAPTER 33

Annie

We've been walking outside for a few hours, and it's getting cold. Josh has been at my side, and I look over at him.

"Are you hanging in there?" I ask.

"Mom, you've asked me that like five times already."

"I know. I just worry."

"I know, but nothing's changed. Leah was gone before, and she's gone now, and she's never coming back."

"Maybe the service tomorrow will be good," I say. "Like a chance to really say goodbye."

"Except there's no body," he says, looking over at me. "She's cremated."

"How do you feel about that?" I ask him.

He shrugs. His hair is short, cropped, dark. His profile just like his father, he's got to be six inches on me now. It's so strange to look up at your child, someone who used to live inside of you, beneath your ribcage, under your heart. It feels like a part of him still lives there.

"I worry about you, Josh."

"I know, Mom, but you don't have to worry right now, not about me. We just got to focus on Jubilee."

We walk like that, one foot in front of the other through the woods, past the tree house. My heart skips a beat looking up at it high in the big oak, remembering when David and James built it ten years ago when the boys were little.

"Remember how you were scared to climb to the top?" I ask him.

He looks over at me with a smirk. "Hey, don't spread rumors like that."

I laugh. "It's the truth. I remember everything."

"Everything?" he says.

"I feel like I remember everything, like the whole time I've been a mother, I just keep storing these memories in glass bottles. I have a cabinet full."

"That's creepy, Mom."

"It's not creepy. It's like my own little apothecary shop, and anytime I'm sad or anxious or worried, I can just pick a different memory and close my eyes, and it's like I'm transported back in time to something happier or funnier or more tender."

"Mom, you're so weird."

I laugh. "I know. It's kind of a part of my job description."

The moment is easy, Josh and me walking side by side, and I'm so grateful for it. Of course, I'm not grateful for the circumstances that have brought us together. But for so many months, he's been so withdrawn, so sad, and even though nothing has changed for the better, I do believe having an answer about where Leah is will give him some sense of solace. I know what would really ease his mind is to know who had taken her in the first place, who took Jubilee.

Just then, a horn blares.

Before we went out, Detective Montgomery told us he'd sound it when the designated time for the search was up. Of course, people are free to continue looking, but there have been certain times earmarked for a group effort. Josh frowns.

"We were supposed to be out for three hours. It's barely been two."

"What is it about, you think?" I ask Josh.

"Let's go find out."

We walk back toward the house, and twenty minutes later, we're sitting on the front porch, listening to Montgomery speaking to everyone who's gathered.

"Thank you all for coming out. It's getting dark, and we have some new evidence to move forward on. I thank everybody for their effort. I know you'll be posted, and we'll let you know if there is another search happening in the morning. Again, thank you so much."

Our friends from church begin clearing out, and I see James speaking with a police officer, Andrew at his side. Montgomery joins them, and David, too.

"Should we go see what's going on?" I ask Josh.

"Just wait, Mom. I'm sure they can handle it. They will ask you to come over if they want you to."

"You don't think they want a woman over there?"

He scoffs. "Mom, that's not what I was saying at all."

But I wonder what he truly means. If the things that have formed his opinion of the world, the way we've raised him, with me in the kitchen and his dad out at work, has caused him to think of me as *less than*.

I frown, wondering about this and not liking where it leaves me. I think how earlier today, David told me everything would be fine and I trusted him, or how I have questions about hiring Robert and he told me there was nothing to worry about. I know it could seem like a small thing, but in this moment it feels important.

Have I been playing small my whole life? It that why I wanted Jubilee in the first place, because I didn't know who I was if I wasn't a mother? I push the thought away, knowing it has no purpose here. Doubting my role in this world in the middle of a crisis is selfish and absurd.

A moment later, David walks over to us with Andrew and James.

"What happened? What's going on?" I ask.

James clears his throat. "I don't want to upset you, Annie."

"Just say it. What?"

"The evidence Montgomery mentioned, well, Andrew found something."

I press a hand to my heart. "What did you find, Andrew?"

It's a shock to see this boy of mine with tears in his eyes. I can't think of the last time I saw him cry. Years maybe. He reached puberty and became a rock, solid through and through. Now he cracks.

"Andrew, are you okay?" I ask, reaching out for his hand.

And that boy who would usually flinch, lets me take it. He squeezes my hand, and then shockingly, he wraps his arms around me.

"Mom," he cries, his shoulder shaking. "We found a pink ribbon. We found . . . We found Jubilee's hair tie. It was out there." He pulls back, his eyes on mine. "It was a few miles from the cornfield. We went out . . . We went out to where Leah was found. I mean, not totally close, but ..." He looks over at his grandpa. "We were wandering those fields. Everybody was divided up, you know that, and well, it was out there."

I feel Josh tense. Andrew steps back, wiping his eyes as if realizing his moment of vulnerability was out of character. James claps his hand on Andrew's back.

"You did good, son, you did good."

I look at David, my throat tight, constricted, and I don't know what words to use, but I'm scared. Scared of what this means, what it means for my little girl. Josh, though, has words.

"We have to find who did this, who took her. Mom, we can't back down. We can't let this break us. We have to find whatever sicko has been hurting the people we love."

I look at David, the name *Robert* on my lips, but I'm not going to mutter it right here, right now. It's not the place and it's not the time.

"It's been a long day, everyone, I think we should call it a night, go inside, get some food and rest. We'll be out looking for her tomorrow in daylight." I walk into the house with my sons, pausing before I go up the porch steps, and turning back to my father-in-law. I wrap my arms around James. "Thank you," I say. "For being with Andrew tonight, for, I don't know, all of it."

"Of course, Annie."

"Are you and Sarah going to come over for dinner?" I ask.

"Is that what you'd like?"

I nod. "Yeah, that'd be good. I made stuff for sloppy joes. It'll be easy if you guys want to come over in a half hour or so." I wipe my eyes and turn away, going into the house.

Emily is in the kitchen. Her brothers are filling her in on everything that we just talked about outside.

"Oh, Mama," she says, her eyes sad. She shouldn't be sad right now. She should be happy. She's engaged to be married in a few months. And instead of planning the wedding shower and the reception, we are looking for her little sister. It all feels twisted and sick. Emily's over the stove, warming up the ground beef in the sauce her grandma canned last summer.

There's a bag of hamburger buns, and Jaden is coming in the back door with a twelve-pack of root beer and an apple pie. "My mom insisted I bring it over," he says.

"Thank you," I say.

"You don't mind if I'm here?"

I shake my head. "Emily needs you. Family stays together, you know?"

He nods, giving me a quick hug as he passes me in the kitchen before going over to Emily and giving her a kiss on the cheek. Andrew and Josh have moved to the living room with David. They're talking quietly with their dad. Knowing that my in-laws won't be here for a few minutes and that Emily's got dinner set and my husband has the boys covered, I excuse myself.

I walk to Jubilee's bedroom and I shut the door. I sit down with my back behind it, taking in the space I curated for a little girl I didn't even know but had dreamed about. I feel like I made a big mistake bringing her here, only for her to be taken. My intentions were good and pure, to extend the love I have in my heart to another, but I have this feeling in the pit of my stomach, wondering if maybe all of this was for selfish gain. That thought rings in my ears and I don't like it, not one bit.

I think of Lisa, how she keeps having child after child to soothe any pain in her life, any problems in her marriage, any questions or doubt about her role in this world. How Susannah judged Lisa so harshly for even considering having another baby to replace the daughter she's just lost. But was I doing anything different when I brought Jubilee home? Soothing the ache in my heart, knowing that my only daughter was going off to get married, that my sons were growing up and leaving, just like Elijah already had.

I know I have nothing to do with Jubilee being kidnapped or taken or whatever's happened to her, but I did change the course of her life. Choosing to bring her here meant she didn't go somewhere else. Maybe in my desire to extend my role in childrearing, I have taken Jubilee down a path that will lead to her death.

None of the other girls have been found. Leah's body was the only one discovered. I close my eyes, panic in my chest, wondering what Jubilee's fate will be, and hating the idea that I've played God in a little girl's life.

CHAPTER 34

Jubilee
One day earlier

The peaches are gone. I saved some of the juice, but that's it. I don't have any water. Nothing to keep warm besides my coat. What I really want right now is a hug.

I'm scared. Scared in my bones that I will be stuck here forever. Lost and alone.

Someone is above me, I hear them. I stand, screaming in the dark, but my voice is hoarse and my sobs overtake me. "Please, help, help me . . ."

But no one comes, and no one helps, and I wonder if this is how I will die.

I wanted to go to Emily's wedding. I wanted to meet Elijah in real life, not just on FaceTime on the iPad. I wanted to plant the garden with Grandma, to can her famous bread-and-butter pickles.

I want my new mom to wrap her arms around me tight and kiss my cheek and tell me everything is going to be okay.

I would say sorry for running away. For leaving late at night. I would say sorry for everything.

But I don't know if any of that will ever happen. Because I am in the dark, underground, and no one has any idea where I am.

CHAPTER 35

Annie

Law enforcement is doing their job today, running Jubilee's hair ribbon through forensics, hoping there might be a fingerprint, a lead. They have marked off the area where James and Andrew found the ribbon itself, scouring that field for more clues that aren't linked to Leah but instead might be linked to Jubilee.

Our household is moving at a slower pace than we have the last few days, because this morning we are preparing to go to Leah's memorial service. I walk into Josh's bedroom and find him struggling with a tie.

"Let me help," I say, making a Windsor knot by memory, having tied enough of David's over the year before. "You look nice," I tell him. And he does. His eyes are sorrowful, but he looks strong and resilient. "Leah loved you so much."

He swallows, his Adam's apple bobbing. "And I loved her, too," he tells me, the tenor of his voice so sad it feels like my heart is breaking all over again.

I remember the day we heard that Leah had been gone missing. It felt so strange, so unexpected. We had just been celebrating her birthday, and the next day she vanished.

No one thought she would run. That wasn't the kind of girl she was. She left her home without telling anyone where she was going and never came home. Josh was distraught, thinking the worst immediately, knowing that someone like Leah wouldn't have gotten in a car with a stranger, wouldn't have done something stupid. That someone must have hurt her, taken her.

"I'm sorry that you were brought into the police station a few days ago for questioning," I say to him, standing behind him and looking in the full-length mirror in his bedroom that hangs on the closet door.

"It's fine," he says. "Like I told the cops, I'm glad if anything I said might help. That's all I want for Leah, for Jubilee, for all those other girls. The consensus seems to be that the cases are linked."

With that line of thinking, it's impossible to not see a bigger link, the link with David and his company.

But I don't want to think about that, not right now, not on a day when we're supposed to be honoring a young girl whose life was taken much too soon, taken by a means we still don't understand.

As a family, we leave the house and pile into our van, heading out to church. All of us have dressed in black. We've been going to Good Fellowship since before we started having kids. It's the church where David grew up, and where we got married. It's where our family has always attended, along with my in-laws.

Now we're in the fifteen-passenger van. James and Sarah have joined us, assuming the parking lot would be full today and it'd be easier to just park one car. I turn on a CD of classical music. The van's old, not connected to any sort of Bluetooth system, and while the teenagers grumble about that a lot, right now it's nice to have the calm music cascading over us. None of us are in the mood to talk. There is so much weighing on our minds.

Emily, though, speaks up. "Jaden is going to meet us there. I mean, I'm sure everyone in town will be there."

I turn around and look at her. She's sitting in the first row of the van next to Sarah, and she looks so grown up, her wedding only a few months away. A young woman, nineteen years old, so much of her is strong and capable, but with my own reflections last night in Jubilee's room, thinking about my choices, how motherhood has utterly defined me, I wonder if being a wife is going to define her similarly. It's not that I don't want that for her; I want her to have all the happiness in the world. But a part of me wonders if she's setting her sights too narrow, too soon.

If this choice to marry a man at such a tender age will form the rest of her life in a detrimental way, of course, it's not something I could ever say aloud, ever speak about. I'm not going to deter her from marrying the man she says she loves. And he loves her back, and it's sweet and it's young and it's new and fresh and alive. And I *want* her to feel that, that aliveness that comes with falling in love.

The early years of my marriage were beautiful. All of my marriage has been beautiful, but those especially. I don't want to take those away from my daughter by weighing in on her decision. After all, it's obvious that she's making choices based on what she knows of me, her mom, marrying young, having babies, staying in the same place . . . the same house, forever.

"What is it?" she asks.

I shake my head. "Just thinking."

She nods, understanding. I turn back around in the seat, looking straight ahead, scared to look back at those rows of my children, scared to look over at my husband, wondering who I am apart from any of the people in this vehicle.

And knowing the answer is quite simple and succinct: nothing. This van, minus Jubilee and Elijah, composes the entirety of my life, practically my entire world. There is a tightening in my chest at the thought. I hate that I'm thinking about myself at a time like this when my mind should be on everyone else, on Leah, on Jubilee.

I squeeze my eyes shut, scared at the thoughts running through my head, scared at the idea that maybe I've made choices that weren't the ones I really wanted to make. But knowing do-overs don't exist, right now, the only thing I have is this present moment. I've already made my choices. I made those choices so early in life that they defined my forever.

It's not that I even have something I want to do differently. It's just the realization of why I brought Jubilee home, knowing it was because I was so scared of what it might mean to not have a child to raise anymore. A surge of shame runs through me at that, thinking it wasn't fair. Maybe if I had sorted out myself before going through with the adoption, maybe — well, not maybe, most certainly — she wouldn't have been kidnapped.

We get to the church, and the heaviness I'm feeling just amplifies as I walk through the corridors into the sanctuary and find a seat and listen to the pastor talk about Leah. As I watch Lisa cry, as I exchange glances with Susannah, the sorrow knits across all of our hearts, a string of invisible yarn tethering us to one another. Josh sits next to me, and I hold his hand. I don't care if he is fifteen years old and someone might think it is awkward. There's nothing that feels awkward in this moment. The emotions are so beyond that. It has no place here.

We listen as Pastor Craig shares a sermon, and then as Leah's older sister speaks. We listen as they open the mic for anyone to say words about Leah, and I am surprised to see Josh stand and walk forward.

I look over at David, both of us not expecting Josh, who is usually reserved, to take center stage. But he does. In his suit and tie, he walks with grace, composure. And even if my life and my world have been small, they've created something so great. I see that so clearly as he stands behind the podium, clearing his throat, speaking words from his heart.

"Leah was my best friend," he said, "ever since we were kids, we were together. Our moms would call us two peas in a pod, even though we were a boy and a girl and looked nothing alike, obviously." He smiles. "I was the dork. She was the princess. Everyone knows that." He looks over at the photograph of her on the easel. "It's obvious, right? Leah is pure beauty, pure grace, and maybe that's weird to say, because she was my best friend, but it feels like she was so much more. It feels like Leah could have been my forever. I'm sorry if that's not appropriate to say," he says, nodding at Lisa and Leah's father, "but it's the truth."

"I loved that girl in a way that feels protective, like I'd do anything for her. I still would. And I still will. I will find the person who did this if it's the last thing I do. I promise you that. Leah deserves justice, just like my little sister Jubilee does. I'm not making this about Juju today. I'm making it about Leah, but I need everyone to know — I won't back down and I hope you don't either, because I loved this girl, and it breaks my heart that she's gone. But I won't let it happen again."

He doesn't cry. He doesn't falter. He speaks with authority, a strength I'm shocked to see. But pride swells my chest as he walks down the steps and walks over to Lisa and gives her a hug, and then Leah's dad, John, gives him a hug. And everybody's crying in the whole church.

Everyone but Josh. His eyes are glassy, but they're not filled with tears.

They're filled with resolve.

CHAPTER 36

Leah
Six days earlier

When Carrie walks out of the bathroom, she shakes her head ever so slightly. I know what she's explaining: that she wasn't able to throw up. Beth, though, nods. Same with Lindy and Tamara.

I give Carrie a hug. And in her ear, I whisper, "It's okay. We'll wake you up, we promise. We're all getting out. We're all getting out alive."

We lie down in our bunk beds, and I tell myself that this is the last time I'm lying in this bed. I don't care what's going to happen next, but I am sure of it. I mostly feel stupid that I didn't do this sooner, throw up my food, but I couldn't have done it alone. I need the help of all of the sisters to make this work. If Mother really has a gun, and she's carrying it when she walks in here, I'll need backup.

Tamara's bed is across from mine, both of us on bottom bunks. Our eyes lock. There are five of us down here, but she and I have a connection I don't have with the rest. A know-ing. And I don't know why it took her six months to get to the point where she would be ready to run, where all the girls would be, but none of that matters now.

The past, it doesn't matter. All that matters is the present. This moment. This very moment.

We lie on our backs and we close our eyes, all of us pretending to sleep. Carrie might already have drifted off. I don't know how much of the medicine got in any of our systems, but I'm hoping that when I close my eyes, it won't push me into to sleep. That instead, I'll be able to stay alert, lucid, and ready.

I can't look over and open my eyes to look at the alarm clock. Because if my eyes open, that will possibly alert someone who is watching that we're not asleep and that it's not a safe time for Mother or Father to come down here.

I try to count the minutes, but I lose track.

A lot of time must have passed, because eventually I hear something, a click.

I roll to my side. Tamara's eyes find mine once more. My heart pounds. We both stayed awake.

We have to move, and we have to move now.

I hear someone in the kitchen, opening and then closing the fridge. I get out of bed. I set up my feet on the floor, and Tamara does the same. I reach under my clothes for the arrowhead pressed to my chest. I fist it.

We don't have other weapons. We couldn't exactly discuss what we would use for protection. But what were we going to use anyway, a plastic fork? A sewing needle? Sure, a needle could have given a prick, but we need a lot more than that.

Tamara stands, too. We know we have to move quickly. I walk to the other beds. Beth and Carrie are out cold. Tamara realizes it. I jostle them, but it's to no use. Tamara is next to Lindy, trying to wake her. She is deeply asleep, too.

Damn it, I think, I took too long in the shower. If I would've been faster, if I hadn't rinsed my hair, if I . . . It doesn't matter. I can't think like that right now. We have to move.

It's just Tamara and me, together. And we walk side by side to the bedroom door, and we pull it open, knowing that whatever is on the other side is going to determine our fate.

We get lucky. Her back is to us, Mother. But she hears the door open, and she makes a move to turn, and her eyes meet mine. And I want to scream. I want to shout. Strangle her. A venom rises within me, and I want her to feel the bite, I want to hurt her the way she has hurt us.

But *her*.

I didn't think it was her.

I thought I knew who'd been kidnapping the girls.

And I thought wrong. I thought so, so wrong.

"You're a monster," I say, barreling toward her, catching her off guard. She thought we were sitting ducks, but she thought wrong.

She is not our mother.

We are someone else's daughters, and we are ready to fight back.

The gun the girls say she always carries is at her side. Tamara dives for it, and I shove Mother to the ground.

"Get off of me. Don't! You were supposed to be asleep. Why didn't you fall asleep?"

I take her wrists in my hand, straddling her. Tamara grabs the gun.

"Do it," I say, "Just shoot her. Just shoot her."

"I don't know how to shoot a gun!" Tamara screams.

I look down at Mother, wanting her dead now. Wanting to never see her face.

But before Tamara shoots, a man is in the doorway. It must be Father.

And he's pulled a trigger.

Tamara falls as a bullet hits her back, blood everywhere.

"No!" I scream, my thoughts a jumbled mess of shock and horror and pure hate. I pull the gun from her hands, pointing it at Mother.

"I'm going to kill her," I say.

"Like hell, you will," he shouts.

The noise must have woken the other girls, because Lindy is in the kitchen now. She's screaming. "Tamara! No, no, no, not Tamara!"

But Tamara has fallen over. The bullet hit her deep. Blood stains her dress, and I roll away, knowing I can't stay.

Lindy rushes towards Tamara, Father and Mother rushing toward Lindy.

And me?

I run out the door, a gun in my hand, fear in my heart. I don't want to leave them there like that; poor Lindy, and Carrie, and sweet Beth. And Tamara is gone, and all I know is Mother and Father are psychotic, monsters in their own right.

I need is to run as far as I can, far, far away. And I begin to move, my legs shaky as I dart through their house.

And I want Josh.

I want Josh.

I don't see anyone as I run out of the house.

When I run out the back door, I hear him, Father, on my heels.

I turn, and I point the gun, and I shoot. I don't hit him, but I just keep running. I'm going to run until I get to the police station, and I'm going to keep on running, because I can't stop and talk to a family member, or a neighbor, or anybody else.

I just need to go to the police. I need to get my sisters free.

I keep running. I keep running through the fields, towards the corn fields, until I can't run anymore. Because he can run faster, because he's wearing shoes, and he hasn't been medicated for months on end. And I am faint, and I am falling, tripping over the dress, over my feet, into the dirt, into the ground. The cornstalks surround me as he tramples on me, shoving his booted foot against my stomach.

"You are a monster!" I scream, "Just like Mother. You're so . . ."

He has a rock raised in his hands, over his head, ready to smash down on me. His foot snaps my wrist, the hand holding the gun limp. In my other hand is the arrowhead. I clutch it. *Josh, where are you?*

I see it, the way he has the rock is aimed at me. And I know what is going to happen.

There's a split-second moment where I know that this is it, this is the end. And Tamara's gone, and now I'm gone, too.

He smashes the rock against my face. Again and again, with a force that takes my breath away, until the fight I had earlier in the basement is gone, until there is nothing left.

The rock slams against my eye sockets and my nose and teeth, and I don't see anything. I don't feel anything. I am gone.

When I went down to that basement, I believed in a very black-and-white version of heaven and hell. And as the gun he was holding goes off — not once, but several times — and as the light of my life goes out, I realize I don't believe in any of that, at all. And maybe I never did.

As I die, all I see is love, love, love. *I love you, Josh. I love you, sisters.*

I don't know what happens after life, after death. And wherever I'm floating, wherever I'm going, my mind is fading fast. Still, something is beating on. Not my heart, of course. But something is beating, nonetheless.

Hope. H-O-P-E. Hope.

My hope is in those corn fields, floating somewhere in the atmosphere.

I hope it falls on the right person, the right sister.

And I hope all of us, somehow, in some version of time or space, are free.

CHAPTER 37

Annie

After the memorial, everyone gathers in the church's hospitality room for coffee and cookies. It feels strange to be sitting at a table with a paper cup of coffee when my daughter is missing, when Lisa's daughter is dead.

"I got to get out of here," I whisper to Emily. "This is just too much, too much sadness. We need to be doing something."

She squeezes my hand. "Mom. The police are doing something. What exactly do you think you're going to do right now? Just walk up and down every street in town?"

I exhale softly. "I don't know, but this feels like torture."

Just then, my mother-in-law walks over to me. "Have you heard?"

"Heard what?" I ask. Emily's eyes furrow in confusion.

"There's another article that just came out, that reporter. It's in the paper, online."

"Are people talking about it here?"

She nods. "That's how I heard about it. Tori Breaker just told me. She sent me the link."

"Forward it to me," I say.

Sarah pulls her phone from her purse, and a moment later my phone buzzes. I open the link and scan the headline. "Local construction company potentially linked to missing girls."

"Oh, my goodness," I say. "This can't be happening."

But it is. As I begin to read the article, I realize how detrimental this is going to be for David and James. "Have they seen it yet?"

Sarah shakes her head. "I don't think so. They're over in the corner, talking to some other men. I think if they'd known, they wouldn't want to be here right now."

"Where do you think they'd want to be?" I ask her.

"I think they'd want to be knocking down Tom Claymore's door and giving him a piece of their mind."

As I read the article, I understand what she means. Claymore doesn't just insinuate a link between the missing girls and David's construction company, he nearly states it outright. People must have read the article, though. It must be circulating now, because I feel eyes on me, a feeling I didn't have a few minutes ago.

It's when Lisa fixes her gaze on mine that I realize this is about to go sideways. I see the anger as she walks toward me, her hands clenched, her eyes steely.

But she walks right past me, not even giving me a second glance, and heads towards David. I follow her.

"Is it true?" Lisa asks him. "Is it true?"

"Is what true?" David says.

"The article, what Tom Claymore wrote. Please tell me you didn't have anything to do with this."

"I knew nothing. I know nothing."

Lisa pulls out her phone and shoves the article in his face. "Then how does Tom Claymore seem to have all the information?"

"I don't know what Tom's saying," David says. Looking past Lisa, he sees me. I press my lips together, not knowing what to do, wanting Pastor Craig to come over and help de-escalate the situation. But Jaden is there before anyone else has a chance to say things they'll regret.

"Hey, Lisa, David, let's not do this here," Jaden says. "This service is for Leah, not for . . ."

"I know it's for Leah," Lisa says. "She's my daughter. That's why I am doing this, for justice. If you knew that Robert was a criminal, how could you ever let him come near—"

Jaden, though, cuts her off. "Lisa, Robert is innocent. He has an alibi. He was released this morning."

"No," Lisa says, "that's not possible. He had to have known. He had to have been a part of it. He had . . ."

"Lisa," Jaden repeats, "he's innocent."

"How can you be so sure?

"He was at the Big Ribbon Diner the night Jubilee went missing."

"All night long, he was there?" Lisa asks. "Because you don't know the exact hour that Jubilee was gone."

"Well, that's the thing. I guess Robert's been going to school online, and he was there for hours all night long, drinking black coffee, eating apple pie and working on schoolwork. Had his computer out and everything. There's camera footage. A waitress verified it. He's clear. He had nothing to do with Jubilee."

"I don't understand," Lisa says. "If he's our only lead, and maybe the cases aren't connected, maybe . . . Maybe . . ."

But then Lisa looks at David, her eyes narrowing. "Or maybe it wasn't Robert at all. Maybe it was someone else. Huh? Someone else on your crew. Someone like you."

"Hey," Jaden says, "we're not going to accuse anyone right now. Do you understand me?"

"I understand nothing," Lisa says. "At this point. I understand absolutely nothing."

* * *

David paces the living room. He has been for hours. That and slamming the front door to pace the porch.

I'm in the kitchen trying to put together spaghetti for dinner, but my mind is racing. My heart is pounding. Everything feels unraveled, and uncertain, like my life is not the one I remember.

When did this happen? Before or after Jubilee came home? I don't think it matters. What matters is the present, and right now everything is a mess.

The article that came out this afternoon paints David and his construction business in a terrible light. He was ranting about suing for slander on the entire drive home from the memorial service. James nodded along, throwing in his two cents, which were just adding fuel to the fire. I kept my mouth shut, because yes, it's horrible what the article said, linking the missing girls to David and his business, but all of that seems to be on the periphery.

The true reason my heart is pounding is that Leah is dead and Jubilee is missing, and I am no closer to the truth than I was the morning when Juju wasn't in her room where she was supposed to be.

The statistics say the odds of ever finding her alive are slim, but I can't give up hope. I have to find meaning in this mess, somehow, some way.

Josh finds me in the kitchen. "Mom, nothing feels right," he says.

"Honey, I know. It's been a big day and you were so brave at the service, the things you said, the words you spoke. It was beautiful. It was a true gift to Leah's life."

"It doesn't feel like a gift when we haven't found the person who did this to her."

"I know," I say. The front door slams again.

Josh winces. "I've never seen Dad so pissed," he says, under his breath.

"It's all so much," I agree. "This is one stress on top of another. It's all compounded. His daughter is gone, and now his business is in shambles."

"Who keeps calling?" Josh asks.

"All the clients; cancellations left and right. He keeps pulling out his day planner and just crossing out the jobs he had lined up for the next six months."

My son whistles under his breath. "What can we do?"

"We can clear his name, and then convince the newspaper to write a story that paints your father in a better light."

His eyes narrow. "You don't think . . ."

"Josh," I say, taken aback, because I know what he's thinking. I'm not truly shocked, though, because I've been thinking it too.

"Could Dad be . . . Did you see him after you went to bed the night Jubilee went missing?"

"I don't know," I say, not wanting to say the truth out loud. A truth so damning it might ruin any life I can still hold onto. But I know David did not come to bed with me that night. He went to his office to work, and I was asleep when he came to bed, and I have no clue what time that might have been.

I go on, saying, "I don't keep track of when he's gotten up in the middle of the night, or anything like that."

"So you're saying there's a chance?"

"A chance of what?" I ask.

"That he might be the one who . . ."

"Josh," I say. The water has begun boiling, and I pour a box of spaghetti into the pot. The sauce is simmering in a pan next to it. "Don't go there."

"Why?" he says. "You're telling me you're not thinking it?"

"I'm telling you it doesn't matter."

"I'm telling you it *does* matter, Mom, because we have to find Jubilee. What are you going to do about it?" he asks me.

"I thought you were the one who was going to find answers," I say, remembering his words at the memorial.

"Maybe I am, by giving you the pep talk you need to do something drastic. If it's not Dad, then who is it?"

"I don't know," I say. "He mostly hires day workers, and . . ."

"Let's go through those names. I'm sure I can Google them. Maybe they were working for Dad for one day and never came back. But maybe there's someone who keeps returning."

"And maybe it's all a weird coincidence. Maybe we're forgetting to look in a more obvious place."

"I hope you're right," he says, "but I'm going to go through his office and find records of who he's hired. I know the police took lots of stuff, but there's got to be something in there I can use."

"I love you," I tell him, as he walks out of the kitchen. I press my lips together, trying to stay steady and not begin to spiral out, just because Josh is making accusations about his dad.

David storms into the kitchen, startling me. "Another one canceled. That job up north. An architect had drawn up the house plans. I spent weeks on that project, and they're dropping me like I'm nothing."

"It will turn around," I say.

"I hope so." He clucks his tongue. "But it's not that simple, Annie. It's done. The article's printed. Rumors are spreading. Everyone thinks I did this. That I kidnapped my own daughter and am . . . what? Hiding her in the attic? And that I did that to other girls, too? Leah? No. It's sick and twisted, and I don't want to do a job for anybody who even entertains the idea that I might have done something so horrific. I'm going to go take a shower," he says.

"All right," I tell him, knowing nothing I say right now will soothe his worry. "Dinner will be ready soon."

He walks out of the kitchen, and I look back at the noodles, feeling like I'm about to boil over too. When they're done, I empty them in the colander and stir the sauce in. No one is around. Emily is with Jaden, and Mason and Andrew are out with friends. Josh is on a mission, doing something I don't quite understand. I'm alone. I reach for a bowl and fill it with the pasta, scooping a few meatballs on top, some grated Parmesan cheese.

Alone at the table, I take a bite, feeling sick to my stomach as I do. Jubilee is alive, God willing, and if so she's somewhere alone, cold, scared . . . and here I am in my warm house, at a big empty table set for one, wondering where I've gone wrong. I know that's a part of a mother's role, taking on the guilt for everything and everyone. That's not my responsibility and it's definitely not fair, but it remains my truth.

It's not my fault Jubilee's not here. Yet I can't help but feel like I could have done more, protected her better, made sure the windows were locked, gone to her room that night to make sure she understood just how loved she was. Because before she was kidnapped in the woods, she had chosen to pack a backpack and exit through the window.

She made that decision, as far as I can tell, and somewhere along the way, she was snatched. Tears fall down my cheeks as I eat the pasta. I need more than food. I need a plan, anything to give me a clue.

I watch as Andrew, Mason and Josh dish up food for themselves and sit on the couches with it, turning on a sports game. I can't sit and watch. I rinse out my bowl and walk through the back door, into the brisk night air. I look up at the stars, wondering if Jubilee is outside or if she is locked up somewhere, if she's warm or if she's cold, if she's scared or if she's brave.

The sky is so big and so vast, so dark. I'm desperate for some answers. A star to wish upon, but everything feels so empty, so bleak. I walk around the house, seeing David's truck in the driveway. I look back up at the house. It's quiet, mostly dark.

I walk to his truck, and the driver door is unlocked. I slip inside it and sit down in his driver's seat. This is the truck he takes everywhere with him. When he's not home, he practically lives in it. It's become a multipurpose office. Lots of days he does invoices and orders supplies while on site.

Poking around it is none of my business and something I've never done before, but before I can stop myself, I am rooting around the truck. It's not that I want to be proven right or wrong, but it's a compulsion, a need for answers.

The console in the center is full of receipts, empty to-go cups and change. In the backseat, there's a hoodie, a few pairs of work boots, gloves, a hard hat.

I open the glove box. Inside, I'm surprised to see a gun and a set of keys buried beneath the registration. A gun? I'm scared to touch it. More than anything, I'm surprised that it's here in the open, so easily accessed. I don't know how to operate a revolver, and I'm certainly not going to test it out on my own in the truck, in the dark, but I wish I knew if it's loaded.

The keys, I hold in my hand. There are two small golden keys on the ring. I'm assuming they are to a property somewhere in the county where he's been working or maybe worked a long time ago, and then he just misplaced them. There's no name on the key holder, no indication of what they might unlock, but I slide them in my pocket anyway, wondering if I should take the gun, too.

For what? What am I going to do with a gun? But more important, what is David doing with this?

I exhale, confused. And then I slam the glove box shut with the gun still in it, not wanting anything to do with something I'm not trained to hold. I think about the keys, wondering where they might lead me, where I'd even find a lock to test them out on. I know every nook and cranny of my home.

But these keys will unlock something. But what?

That is the question I need to answer. Now.

CHAPTER 38

Annie

I walk back into my home with the unidentified keys in my pocket. Everything feels unsettled, and with the sunset and the sky turning gray and dark, there's a heaviness looming over everything.

In the house, I see Mason. "Hey, Mom," he says. "Grandma was here and wanted you to come to her place."

"What was it about?" I ask.

He shrugs. "I don't know. She said she was working on something and wanted your opinion."

"All right," I say, passing through the house and heading to the back door. "I'll be back in a bit."

He briefly looks up from the phone in his hand. At fourteen years old, I'm not sure I even want to know what he's looking at, what content he's consuming. As a mother, our minds are always running through a hundred possibilities, always wanting to make sure that the kids are all right. I pray he is. That they all are.

I cross the yard towards Sarah's place and knock on the door. She answers a few minutes later.

"Hey," she says, pulling open the door. "I'm glad you could come by."

"What's it about?"

"Nothing urgent," she says. "I just had been making a new dress for Jubilee before, well, before she went missing, and I thought I would finish it up. But what do you think?" she asks, walking to her sewing room. I follow. "I want to know if you think I should use a full skirt, to her knees or to her calves? What would she like more?"

She has a dress pinned to a pattern on her sewing table. It's a soft, buttery yellow fabric that I know Jubilee will love. It looks like there will be a sash for her waist, a pink ribbon and puffy sleeves.

"She's going to feel like a princess in that. I'd say go longer."

Sarah nods. "All right. I didn't want to make the wrong decision. But it might be easier for her to run if it was shorter."

"True," I say, "but this dress is so pretty, I can't imagine she'll be playing in it too much."

Sarah smiles, running her hand over the fabric. "I'm so sorry," she says, "that we don't know any more than we did a few days ago."

"I haven't lost hope yet," I say. "It's going to be okay. It has to be."

Sarah nods gravely, tears in her eyes.

"Can I ask you something?"

"You can ask me anything," Sarah says.

"You've known me more than half your life. We've both always stayed at home. Do you ever wish you had gotten a job outside of the house?"

She frowns. "I always liked helping James around the property, and then all those years raising David." She smiles. "And then of course him marrying you, and the two of you growing your family with such abundance. I have loved being so close and helping with the kids as they've grown up. I hope you know that."

I nod. "No, I do," I say. "Of course. It's just . . ." I swallow. "Sometimes I wonder about my own life, my choices. About not doing more, not doing something different. If one day I'll wake up and regret it."

Sarah exhales slowly. "This sounds like it calls for a cup of tea."

We walk to the kitchen and she puts on the kettle, reaching for two bags of chamomile tea. "I have some poppy seed Bundt cake. Would you like a slice?"

"Sure," I say.

She cuts us each a piece and places them on plates, carrying them to the table. The kettle whistles, and she pours the hot water into the mugs.

"Do you have any honey?" I ask.

She looks in the cupboard, frowning, and then the pantry that's next to the refrigerator. "I think we must be out, but I know I have some more in the basement pantry. Do you want to go grab it?"

"Sure," I say. I've been down to the pantry probably hundreds of times. We've put up peaches and pickles every summer for over two decades. Made batches of Christmas cookies for friends and family and prepared things like potato salad for cookouts. So opening the door to the pantry that's in the basement and walking down the stairs is second nature.

I flip on the lights and hold the handrail walking down to the basement. The laundry room is down here, too, and I turn to the left where the pantry is. There are rows of our canned goods along with the bulk items she's purchased at Costco: twenty-five pound bags of rice and flour, extra jars of peanut butter and jelly, and oatmeal. She's nothing if not prepared.

I look on the metal racks and find a two-pack of honey. I pull one off and read the label, organic unfiltered. I like my tea sweet, with a little bit of milk, too.

Before I turn to go back up the stairs, I notice the door at the end of the long pantry. I've seen it hundreds of times, but I've never thought about it, assuming it's a supply closet or something. I frown, wondering why I've never looked more closely. I walk over to it. Pulling down the handle, I try to open the door, but it doesn't budge.

There's no lock on it either, which means the lock would be from the other side. But that doesn't make any sense. If it's a closet, the only access point would be from where I'm standing right now. I walk back upstairs, turning off a light and shutting the door.

"Hey, Sarah," I say, carrying the honey to the kitchen counter, unscrewing the cap, and pulling off the seal. "What's the closet down in the pantry go to? I tried to open it out of curiosity, but it wouldn't budge, like it was locked, but from the other side."

"Oh yeah, we never use that. It's a tunnel that goes to the barn."

"What do you mean, a tunnel?"

"Yeah, I mean, this house is 100 years old. I guess at some point, someone wanted to have access from the barn to this house in case of an emergency."

"Well, why don't you have the lock on the other side, on both sides? How do you open that door?"

"There was never a lock. That's the thing, this old house, there's not a lock on the other side either. At some point, James barred off the door from the other side. It's a pretty secure closure, which keeps out the cold air or any animal from getting in the house."

"I see," I say. "That's kind of strange, to have a tunnel between the house and the barn."

She shrugs. "I don't know. Maybe it was helpful in the winters, to get to the livestock."

"That makes sense," I say.

"Or maybe someone with a shovel was just really bored," Sarah says with a laugh. "Anyway, you can access it from the barn. I haven't done that in years, though. I mean, I haven't really done that in forever. Haven't had any need to."

We sit with the tea and cake, and I try to think of what I was wanting to talk to Sarah about before I went down to the pantry because now my mind is blank. It's disturbing thinking of that passageway, something cold, hollow.

"What is it?" Sarah asks.

I shrug. "I don't know. I've just felt off lately, really ever since we brought Jubilee home. But if I'm being really honest, I think I was feeling off even before then, like my motivation for having another child was maybe wrong."

"Oh, Annie, don't say that."

I shrug. "How can I think otherwise?"

"I don't know," she says. "Jubilee is a gift. She's a beautiful girl, and—"

"I know all of that," I say. "But my desire to have another child may have just been me wanting to fill a void in my life."

Sarah lifts the mug of tea to her lips and takes a sip, thinking. "That's a pretty grim way of viewing your life, Annie."

"I know," I say, my voice hushed, embarrassed. "I know how it sounds, like I'm some sort of a monster, like using children as a coping mechanism or something."

"I didn't say you were a monster, but sometimes . . . Well, maybe if you were unsatisfied, you were making choices to fill a hole, but I think most people do that to some degree, with something or another."

"What about you? What do you use?"

"Have you seen how many dresses I sew? I swear, I am constantly making something new."

"Are you bored?"

"Maybe a little bit, but isn't that life? We're just trying to find something to make us happy, keep us going, and raising children is probably better than something more detrimental, like an addiction."

"Well, sure," I say. "But—"

"Maybe you're overthinking it," she said softly.

"Maybe," I say. "But I feel sick inside, like my desire to fill some hole in my heart is what propelled me to bring Jubilee home, and now she's gone, and is this my punishment? For being selfish?"

"No one is punishing you, Annie," Sarah says.

Tears fill my eyes. "I hate that she's gone, and I hate that I didn't do my job as a mom to protect her."

"You're doing everything you can to bring her home safely, and she *will* be home safely."

"Just like Leah?"

Sarah presses her lips together. "You know that's not what I mean."

I exhale, feeling frustrated and lost, like there are no easy answers. Finishing my tea, I carry it to the sink. "Thank you," I say, "for the talk."

"Well, thank you for giving me advice on how I should sew Jubilee's dress."

I smile, giving my mother-in-law a hug and hoping tomorrow goes better than today.

* * *

When I leave Sarah's house, I start walking to my place, but before I do, I pause, thinking about the barn to my left, the key in my pocket. I have lived on this property for over two decades and in all that time, I never knew that there was a tunnel from the barn to the old farmhouse. It's strange, thinking about me living here for so long and that there are still secrets kept buried, things hidden from me, a tunnel that's dark and abandoned, cold and decrepit. It sends a shiver down my spine, and it causes me to head toward the barn. Not because I want to see some abandoned dirt tunnel . . . but I guess I sort of do. I want to know what Sarah is talking about and understand why it was boarded up in the first place.

I pull open the big barn doors. There's no livestock anymore. That was abandoned decades ago. James has always done construction work, even while he was raising David, and the barn is more of a tool shed now than anything, full of their equipment for big projects, piles of lumber. It smells like sawdust and metal, oil and hard work. I've been in here countless times over the years, coming to check in on my husband, letting him know dinner was ready or that he'd lost track of time.

Now, I enter the barn and it's empty. I move to one of the work benches and reach for the cord over my head, pulling on a single bulb, illuminating the space ever so slightly. The rafters are high above my head. There's no hay that fills the loft. Instead, it's boxes that house our Christmas ornaments and our decorations for the Fourth of July.

I walk around the space, looking over every inch of the floor. In the back right corner, besides a tarp covering a riding lawn mower, I find a door in the floor. Bending down to my knees, I discover a padlock, open and set aside, as if it's been forgotten. I pull the key from my pocket, jamming it in the rusty lock. It fits.

My heart pounds, and I don't even know what I'm thinking. The door isn't locked, and I can't see very clearly because it's so dark. I pull open the big, heavy door, lifting it from the floor. The back of the door is covered in a thick layer of insulation, and there's a big hole below.

"Hello?" I call out.

There is no reply. Needing to know what is down there, I stand, looking for a freestanding ladder. I see one that has extensions, in the corner, propped against a wall of the barn. Walking to it, I heave as I take hold of it in both my hands, carrying it to the hole in the floor.

I lower it, scared, extending it as it reaches the ground below. By the time it hits the ground it is fully extended, probably thirty feet.

I pull out my phone and turn on the flashlight, taking my time to carefully maneuver down the ladder until I get to the bottom.

I plug my nose; the smell is overwhelming. Confused, looking around trying to understand, trying to, but it is more clear than I wanted to imagine. Someone has been down here, *living* down here. There are jars of canned food, empty, but that's not what causes me to keel over and vomit. It's what I see drawn on the dirt floor: H-O-P-E.

I heave up the tea and the cake and the pasta, completely overwhelmed, horrified.

"Annie," I hear a voice call out above me in the barn. I tense, trembling, fear coursing through me. I look back to the ladder. The tunnel is long, but at the end, I see another door. I see a wall, not a door, and maybe it's a false door that's been built to ease the noise that may have been coming from this tunnel. From a holding cell for a child, my child.

"Annie." It's David. I see him climbing down the ladder. "What are you doing?"

"I want to get out," I say. "I'm trying to get out of here."

I begin scurrying up the ladder, shoving at him, wanting him back in the barn. I want to be on solid footing, on solid ground. I don't want to be down in that tunnel with my husband. My husband?

"Oh, my God. David," I say. "Was this you? All along, this is you? You took her and put her down here and—"

"What? Put who where?"

"Don't do this," I say. "Don't act innocent. I know what you did. You are just a monster."

"No," David says, his voice calm, sure. "I never have been down there."

"All the time you worked in this barn, you've never gone down the tunnel?"

"Why would I?" he says. "When I was a kid, I knew there was a tunnel between my parents' house and the barn and then, I don't know, a couple decades ago, my dad barricaded it, locked it up. There's nothing down there. Why would I go down there?"

"The key was in your glove box, David. I'm not an idiot. Along with a gun."

"Look," he says. "If the key was in my car, it must have gotten off my keychain somehow. The gun? Yeah, I purchased that a long time ago. I know I told you, but you probably didn't hear that, either; you are so wrapped up in the kids."

"You want to start pointing a finger at me now?"

"Someone was down there. They were words spelled in the dirt . . . Spelling 'hope.'"

David's face goes slack. "I didn't see . . . What are you saying?"

"I'm saying you kidnapped our daughter and put her down there. The key was in your car, David. It was you. It was you."

"I'm calling Jaden," he says.

"I'm calling the cops right now."

"Calm down."

"Don't tell me to calm down," I say, my whole body shaking.

"You got it wrong," he says. "I swear to you, Annie. You got it all wrong."

But I don't think so. The only question I have is, why would my husband do this to our child?

I lock eyes with my husband, the man who has been with me through thick and thin, all the ups and downs of our marriage. "I feel like I don't even know you," I say.

Before David can answer that or turn to climb the ladder back up to the barn to call Jaden, we hear footsteps.

"It's not me," he says. "I swear, Annie. I love you. I love our family. I would never. The fact that you would even think I could be capable of . . ."

"David, you down there?" It's James.

"Yeah, Dad. Just a sec."

We hear his heavy footsteps near the door. And then, a moment later, we see his feet as he begins to climb down the ladder.

"David," I whisper.

"Dad, what do you need?" David asks, but as he asks, it's as if the truth has just dawned on my husband. If he is being honest, and he has nothing to do with Jubilee going missing, all evidence in this tunnel points to James. Has she been here? Where is she now?

Now, I realize it wasn't my husband who took her . . . I think it was my father-in-law. The person who took her had

198

to know about the job sites where David was working. That someone is James.

My heart begins to race as James turns. Now that he's reached the bottom of the ladder, I step forward, wanting David closer, his protection.

But as he turns, I look past him, to the other side of this tunnel. Crouched in a ball, lying on her side, is my daughter.

She's not moving.

A blood-curdling cry escapes my mouth as I rush toward her, past the two men. To my little girl who is lying there, lethargic. I'm terrified that she's gone, that I'm too late.

I pull her toward me, her body frail and weak, limp in my arms, and I cry. And David is next to me, and James, too.

"I'm calling 911," James says, moving into action. He crawls up the ladder quickly. There is intense concern in his voice, concern for his granddaughter, and suddenly I doubt everything I was just thinking.

"David," I say. "I thought . . . were you thinking . . . ?" I don't know how to put it in words, everything I was just thinking. Everything is jumbled, unsure.

"We'll know everything soon enough," David says. He has his hand on Jubilee's wrist, looking for a pulse. His eyes meet mine.

"She's alive. Annie, she's alive because you found her."

CHAPTER 39

Annie

Within minutes, a medical team is here, coming down the ladder, into the tunnel, with a stretcher.

Soon, we're outside. All of us huddle around the ambulance as Jubilee is loaded up. I climb in with her. David tells me he'll take his truck. As the ambulance doors close, I see David and Josh get in his truck. The other members of the family pile into the van. James is at the wheel. I didn't even have time to stop and ask if anyone needed anything.

Right now, my focus is Jubilee.

A medic has already begun giving her an IV. "She's dehydrated," she says, looking down at her. "Hungry, I'm sure. And look, I think her foot's broken."

I see what she means. There are bruises all around her ankle, and it's distorted.

"She probably fell," I say. "I moved that ladder down into the tunnel. That's how I got down. But if she opened that door and jumped in, not knowing it was so deep . . ." I close my eyes.

I thought my own husband was a killer. My father-in-law a potential murderer. I swallow, looking at my little girl, knowing I'm not going to have the complete story until she is alert. But right now, she's breathing.

She's blinking, and her voice croaks. "Mama," she says.

My heart swells as I reach tenderly for her hand.

I don't know why the universe conspired to bring her into my life and mine into hers. And maybe my motives were selfish in some ways. Maybe I've been scared of what it meant to grow up, to not just be a mom, but to find myself. But in this moment, Jubilee's eyes lock with mine and I hold her hand in my palm and I look at her, holding onto that one word.

Mama.

Leah is dead, and there are other girls missing. But Jubilee is alive. Maybe the fact that we have one another is more than enough.

Maybe in the end, it doesn't matter how people come into your life, because if they're meant to stay, they will. And Jubilee is in mine. I feel like this nine-year-old is teaching me more than I ever imagined I'd learn from a child.

She's teaching me what it means to let our hearts expand, to let love in, in a new way.

When we get to the hospital, I sigh with relief as a medical team moves into action, bringing the stretcher into the emergency room.

I'm at her side, and David joins me within a few minutes. I hold his hand. "Look at her foot," I say.

He grimaces. "She must have fallen in there."

"Why wasn't the trapdoor locked?"

He runs a hand over his bearded jaw. "It's probably not been locked for a decade. Nothing's down there except some old jars and garbage. You saw it. Probably random stuff that was left when Dad closed it all up. He always thought it was a dangerous place. It's all dirt, could just collapse."

I shake my head. "But what about the other girls?" I ask. "I really thought it was all linked. All connected."

David walks towards Jubilee and sits in a chair at her bedside as a doctor looks her over. "I don't know, Annie. I don't know where those other girls are. But right now, I have peace in knowing where ours is."

While Jubilee is getting her bone set, I walk into the waiting room to update the rest of the family. Josh gives me a big hug. "You did it, Mom. You found her."

Tears fill my eyes. "But the other girls . . ." I say. "I really thought it was all related. I thought the situation was linked, that . . ."

"I know," he says. "It looks like Jubilee was just running, hiding. Probably went in there and got stuck. Fell and then couldn't get out, and then was too dehydrated to cry for help. And it also means there is still a killer on the loose," Josh says, his eyes steely.

"I know, but . . ."

"No, Mom. We have to find them. We have to find whoever killed Leah and took those other four girls."

"Not tonight," I say. "Tonight, we have peace."

"But we don't have peace," he says flatly. "You heard me at the funeral. I said I would do whatever it takes to get justice for Leah, and I will."

* * *

Hours later, Jubilee is alert, sitting up in bed, and the police are there asking for her story. Detective Montgomery is taking notes about everything.

"Can this just wait till tomorrow?" I ask. "She's a little girl, and she's just woken."

"We need to be sure the case is closed," he says.

"All right," I say, giving in. "Jubilee, are you up for it?"

She nods. "It's my fault," she says, tears in her eyes. "I'm sorry, Mom and Dad. I really am. I just got upset and scared and maybe a little angry. So I packed a bag, and thought I was going to go just up to the tree house. But then I got close and a coyote was there, and I dropped my bag when I was running. I thought I'd come back to the house, but then I thought you might get mad that I'd left. So I thought I'd hide out for just a little bit longer. And I went in the barn, and that was the stupidest thing I ever did," she says, crying.

"I'm so sorry," she continues. "I found that door in the back of the barn when I was looking around, and I opened it and fell in. I fell on my foot really hard, and I couldn't move very much. But Grandma must have had some old food there. She said it used to be her pantry before, Grandpa fixed up a real nice new one for her, in the basement. There were some jars down there, but there wasn't any water. I had peaches. She makes the best peaches, and I drank the peach juice."

"Thank God for that," I say, pressing my fingers to my lip, realizing I'd blamed the wrong people all along: my father-in-law, my husband, Robert Pascal. I was so confused. Did I really even see the word 'HOPE' written in the dirt? Looking back, it seemed so real, but . . .

Maybe it doesn't matter, because everything that happened brought me to the barn, brought me to my daughter. I found Jubilee.

She might not have lived another day.

"I am so sorry, Mama. I'm sorry."

"Don't be," I say. "We're all learning, and I'm just glad you're okay."

"Me too," she says, crying violently.

I look at the detective. "Can we do this later? If you need more information, can we do it tomorrow? She's exhausted."

He nods, realizing that what Jubilee needs right now is sleep. "I'm so glad your little girl came home."

"Me too," I say. "Thank you for everything you did to help us."

Detective Montgomery leaves, and I pull up a chair at Jubilee's bedside. David does, too.

We fall asleep like that, each of us holding our little girl's hand.

Our little girl, who's no longer lost. She's been found.

CHAPTER 40

Josh

I'm lying in my bed, staring at the ceiling, the gun I found in Dad's glove compartment in my hand. I got in the truck before him and saw it open, the gleaming steel just asking to be taken.

So I took it. I need to be ready for when I find Leah's killer.

In my Christmas stocking this year, I got one of those packets of all those glow-in-the-dark stars, and I stuck them to my ceiling. I made constellations. I look at them at night, thinking maybe wherever Leah was, she was looking at them too. I stare at them now.

And I know that was naive thinking, knowing she's really gone, and she's never coming back. Her body isn't just buried. It's cremated. And I wish I had some of her ashes. Maybe that's creepy. I don't care. I'd put them in a pouch and wear it around my neck and I'd have her next to me.

I wish I had the arrowhead. I wish her mom would've given it to me. I know that's probably selfish to want something like that. It's not mine to take. I gave it to their daughter, after all. But still. I look at my ceiling and suddenly, the stars don't seem that big anymore, that far away.

I'm scared. I'm scared of letting her down, even in death. I want to find who did this to her, who hurt her, who put a bullet in her head, who took away her chance at life and love.

And when I was standing up at that funeral, and I told everybody that I would get justice for her, I meant it.

Because if I don't do that, what do I have? Mom found Jubilee, her daughter, and I'm going to find the person who did this to Leah.

I feel like I can do it now, in a way I didn't feel I could before, because I saw what Mom went through, how she wouldn't give up until she found her little girl. And I won't give up until I find peace for Leah, for her family.

And it's funny, because Mom always beats herself up, like she's not doing enough for us kids, like not putting in the time and not making us good enough food and forgetting to switch the laundry or getting gas in the tank, but it's all silly things that she worries about. Because at the end of the day, my mom's amazing. She's a hero.

She's *my* hero. And my chest gets all tight again; the gun is cold.

My phone buzzes, and I reach for it. It's Nathan. "Hey, do you want to meet up?"

"Sure," I say. "What are you thinking?"

"I'll pick you up. We can get tacos or something."

I look at the clock. It's only nine o'clock. Why am I in bed already? Maybe because it's been a hell of a day. "Sure," I say. I slide the gun in the pocket of my jeans, putting on a baggy sweatshirt.

I leave my room and go to the kitchen where Mom and Dad are. "Nathan asked if I wanted to grab some food. Is that cool?"

"Of course," Mom says. "Anything you need, honey?"

It's been a day since Jubilee got back from the hospital, and she's tucked in bed right now, but I know as soon as Mom finishes cleaning the kitchen, she's going to walk down the hall and she's going to sit on the floor next to Jubilee's bed, to lie there until she's sure Jubilee is out cold, sleeping.

Again, that's real devotion. That's real love. I want to believe that's what I have for Leah even now.

"Don't be out too late," Dad says.

"I won't. I'll be home by eleven. Promise."

"All right. Stay safe."

When Nathan pulls up the driveway, I jump in the passenger seat. "My mom let me borrow her car," he says.

"What happened to your car?" I ask him.

He shrugs. "I can't get it to start." He chuckles. "I know, it's a piece of crap."

"It's cool, though, you have a car and a license. I turn sixteen in a few months and still haven't taken driver's ed. I've been so out of it. I haven't had the energy or the motivation to do anything. And now Leah's gone. It just feels worse."

I look behind me in the backseat. There are piles of fabric. "I didn't know your mom sewed."

"Oh yeah, she sews like your grandma. I think they, like, do sewing classes together or something."

"That's cool," I say. We pull out the driveway and head toward town.

"What do you think? Pizza or Taco Bell?"

I laugh. "Taco Bell all the way. You can't beat the 99-cent menu."

Nathan laughs. Before I turn back to look out the front window, something catches my eye. Next to the pile of fabric is a spool of ribbon, a spool of pink ribbon. I pick it up.

"What's that?" Nathan asks, as I spin the ribbon in my finger.

"I don't know. I just feel like I've seen this ribbon before."

"Oh, girly-girl, huh?"

"Shut up," I say, punching Nathan in the shoulder. "No, but honestly, I swear this is the ribbon that they found when looking for Jubilee. Near the cornfields."

"Morbid much?"

"But it wasn't Jubilee's ribbon, was it?" I say. "I mean, that's what my grandpa and brother thought, because they found it near the cornfield, but I bet it was probably Leah's."

"Shit," Nathan says. "This is really dark."

I look at Nathan and wonder if I've been missing something all this time.

"What?" Nathan says.

"I don't know," I say. "It's weird, right, this ribbon being in your mom's car?"

"I don't know. She probably got it at Walmart or something."

"Right," I say.

When Leah was found, she was wearing a homemade dress. Her hair was tightly braided. She had no shoes on. My arrowhead was in one hand, her other hand was unfurled. She'd been shot in the face four times, blood caked everywhere. She was barely recognizable, but her DNA identified her, and she was in a cornfield.

A cornfield that I know for a fact is one mile west of Nathan's house.

"Dude, you got really quiet. What's going on?" he asks.

"Hey, can we actually . . . Can we go to your house for some food? Your mom was always making stuff."

"You don't want Taco Bell?"

"I don't know. What'd you have for dinner?"

He shrugs. "Pasta? I don't know."

"Do you have leftovers?"

"I think so."

"Maybe I could just stay over the night," I say. "What do you think?"

"How about your house?" he asks. "You know my mom doesn't like me to have people over."

"Right," I say. Nathan's never had a sleepover in all the years I've known him. I can count on one hand how many times I have been to his house.

"We should just go to Taco Bell," he says. "My parents hate company."

"Why?" I ask.

"I don't know. You know how they get."

"Not really. How do they get?"

He shrugs. "They always say our house is too small for other people."

I frown. "All right. Taco Bell it is."

We drive to Taco Bell, and I keep messing with that ribbon, thinking about how in all the times I've known Nathan, in — what, ten years? — I've been to his house, maybe two, three times. Susannah always comes to our house. We never go there.

Which is kind of weird, because we are always at Lisa's place, too. Maybe Nathan's right: maybe it is just because they have a small place with one kid, and Mom and Lisa have lots of kids with big properties. Still, the ribbon, the fabric . . . something feels off.

We get the food at Taco Bell and sit in the parking lot and eat our seven-layer burritos and drink our Mountain Dews. "Why doesn't your mom want people over, ever? I mean, I get a whole crowd, but just a friend to spend the night?"

"I don't know. You know how my mom is. She's private. My dad is, too."

"Your dad's a doctor, right?"

"Yeah."

"And your mom, she's never worked?"

"Well, before she had me, I guess she was really into some sort of security job, like the technical side. She developed technology for security systems."

"Is your house all decked out?"

"Oh yeah," Nathan says. "My mom has cameras everywhere. When someone pulls up on the property, there's immediately alarms that go off."

"Huh," I say. "That's pretty cool. Maybe we should have that at our house, and Jubilee wouldn't have ran away."

"You want to check it out?" he says. "We can go to my place and I'll show you the system. Mom will be okay, just this once."

"Sweet," I say, playing it cool, feeling like something is about to click into place.

When we get to Nathan's house, I exhale, because driving past those corn fields always gets me.

"I know, right?" Nathan says, reading my mind. Like I said, we've been friends forever. It's just, it's a more one-sided friendship, him coming to me, Susannah coming to us.

When we get to his house, he points out cameras along the driveway. "See, there's one up there in the tree, and one there on the fence."

"Why is your mom so insistent on high security?"

He shrugs. "I don't know. Like I said, I think it's just her hobby."

When we get to the house, though, it's super quiet. Susannah meets us in the living room. "What are you guys doing here? I thought you were going to get food."

"We did," Nathan says. "We were just talking about security stuff, and I was telling Josh about our security system."

"Oh," Susannah says, smiling. "Did you get enough to eat? It's kind of late. Does your mom want you home?" she asks me.

"It's only ten. They said I can be out till eleven."

"Right," Susannah says. It's only then I notice her eyes dart back to a door down the hall. When she walks away, telling us to make ourselves comfortable, I asked Nathan where that goes.

"Oh, that's the basement."

"What's down there?"

"My mom's canning stuff."

"Oh, my grandma has all her stuff like that in the basement, too."

Nathan shrugs. "I never go down there. I want frozen pizza, not pickled asparagus."

Their house is small, an office and sewing room, Nathan's bedroom and his parents' room, a living room and kitchen. It's probably just 1,200 square feet. When Nathan leaves to go to the bathroom, though, I open the door to the basement and immediately jump down the stairs in three steps.

When I get to the bottom, though, I hear Susannah call to me from the top of landing. "What are you doing down there?"

"Oh, nothing. Just looking around."

"Yeah. Well, it's time to come back upstairs."

Why is she creeping on me like this? My eyes dart around, and I see a camera in the corner. "Oh wow. You have a camera down here, too?"

"Yes, I do," she says, "but you should really come upstairs."

"Okay," I say. But before I do, Nathan's out of the bathroom, standing there with his mom, completely oblivious.

"Hey, Mom. Weird, but in the car, Josh saw this ribbon, like the spool of ribbon. It was pink. Where'd you get that, like, at Walmart? Something like that? Because that's the same ribbon he said was in the cornfield by where Leah's body was found."

I can feel the tension. Nathan has no idea, but I feel it.

The house feels too creepy and empty. I don't even know where his dad is.

His mom's acting skittish. And while she's always played it too cool, too easygoing for my liking, this is next-level. She's acting hypervigilant now.

While they're talking, I scan the room as quickly as possible. Nathan wasn't exaggerating. There are tons of canned food down here. So much. But there's also a door. And when I tug at it, it opens. Inside, I see Terry, Nathan's dad, turning to me, staring.

In his hand is a basket of laundry. "Uh . . ."

I hear Susannah calling, running down the stairs. "Terry, it's fine. It's fine, Nathan. Josh just came over and he got lost, and . . ."

But I'm not lost, I think, looking around this creepy room.

It's like a dollhouse, a whole living-room apartment, with a small kitchenette.

I move past Terry. I see bloodstains on the carpet. "What is this place?"

And then in the bedroom, I see three sets of bunk beds. I flick on the lights.

I see three bodies lying in the bed, all of them wide-eyed as if scared. Something is wrong here. Terribly, sickeningly wrong.

Terry is behind me. And I pull out my phone, before he can do anything, pressing 911.

"Stop what you are doing," Terry says, holding a gun out to me. Behind him Nathan is shouting, telling his dad to stop, and Susannah is looking stunned. But I am no fool. I have a gun, too.

"Don't," Susannah says.

But I do. I must. I tell the operator that I found three little lost girls, lying in beds, hidden in a basement. As I speak, I pull out the gun.

"Don't even think about it!" Terry shouts.

"What is happening? Who are these girls? Your prisoners?"

"It's our family," he says stoically.

"We've been trapped for years," one of the girls whimpers.

My blood curdles in disgust. Terry is coming closer to me, and I'm scared that if I don't do something drastic, he is going to get this gun from me and do something irrevocable with it.

I point the gun at Terry. Then I press the trigger, shooting him in the shoulder.

He falls, stunned.

Susannah shouts, tells me to stop, bending down and reaching for the gun in Terry's hands, pointing it toward me.

That is not how this ends — with them hurting anyone else.

I pull the trigger again, this time shooting my mom's best friend in the shoulder. She falls next to her husband.

I couldn't save Leah, but I can save the other girls down here.

CHAPTER 41

Annie

We get the call from Jaden. "Come quick," he says. "The hospital."

"Oh God," I say. "Was there an accident? Did something happen to Josh?" I look over at David. Josh has been gone for an hour and a half. He hasn't broken curfew or anything, but . . .

"It's worse than that," he says. "Actually, it's worse than you could've imagined."

I don't want to leave Jubilee here, but Emily tells me it's fine. "I'll sit in her bedroom," she promises. "You go find out what happened to Josh, what's going on. Just keep us posted, okay?" Andrew, Mason, Emily, David and I are standing in the living room, where I just told them what Jaden said.

"Go," Emily says. "Now."

"Okay," I say, reaching for my purse. David grabs his keys, and we get in his truck. We drive to the hospital quickly. "I can't believe you had a gun in your glove box. You didn't tell me that."

"I *did* tell you that," he says.

"I feel like there are so many things we haven't talked about in so long."

"I know," he says. "I was probably spending too much time with work."

"And I was probably spending too much time with the kids."

"Look, Annie, there is something I do have to confess. I have been carrying it around for far too long."

"What is it?" I ask, my strength already feeling compromised.

"Six months ago, I got an email from Leah. About a week before she was kidnapped."

"What email?"

"I spoke with the detectives about it, when they went through my things. I didn't want to hide anything. But I just didn't know how to tell you, not while we were still looking for Jubilee."

"What was the email?"

"She thought I was the kidnapper. She pieced things together, after doing a report on the local missing girls for a school project. She saw the job sites on the corkboard in my office when she and Josh were studying in there one afternoon. She thought she had put things together."

"Why didn't you say something, earlier, to me?"

"What would I say? The email was full of wrong information, and it would have . . ."

"I can't believe you have been carrying all that on your own. I feel like this is part of our problem. We aren't being honest with one another, communicating about our lives."

He reaches for my hand, between our car seats, and squeezes it. "We can improve. I want to be closer to you. I want to know your heart, Annie."

"Are we going to be okay?" I ask him, the man who has always been my vision of forever.

"I hope so," he says, lacing his fingers with mine.

I'm so sorry I ever doubted him, but I didn't know what to believe. Everything felt lost and jumbled, and I still don't know exactly who I am and where I'm going to go, and who I want to be separate from being a mother.

But I do know this: I love being David's wife, and I love being a mom. And I know I want a little bit more, but I have the support of a family to fight for those dreams, to figure them out.

It doesn't all have to happen right now. It doesn't have to happen today. Eventually, it will. And when it does, it will be big and bright and beautiful. And it will be mine. It will be ours.

David parks truck at the hospital, and he looks at me before we get out of the car. "Whatever happens," he says, "we're in it together." And he kisses me quickly on the lips. And even though it's just a second long, it's like I see a movie flash before my eyes of the last twenty-five years. The two of us, we are in it together, fighting for our happily ever after.

And side by side, we walk into the emergency room, the room we were in just a day ago.

Jaden is there, and so are other officers, and there are reporters outside.

I shake my head, confused, scared. "What's going on?"

Jaden brings me to Josh's room. He's lying in a bed, alert.

"What happened?" I say, "Was there a car accident? Was . . ."

"No," he says, "they have me here just to make sure I'm not going to fall apart."

"Fall apart over what?"

"I found who killed Leah."

"What?" I ask, pressing a hand on my heart, gasping, looking at David and then Jaden, and then back at my son. "Who? What? What happened?"

"All that time, all those girls," he said, "it was Terry and Susannah."

"What?" My stomach drops, shock racing through my body. "What do you mean, Terry and Susannah?"

Jaden nods. "They had a room in their basement, a whole apartment. The girls had been kept there."

"Nathan knew?" I ask.

Jaden shakes his head. "I don't think so. I think he was oblivious. The room was locked, there was a security surveillance system, and his life was so sheltered . . . a different kind of sheltered than ours."

"Oh my God," I say. "No, this can't be true. This can't be true."

"It is, Mom," Josh says.

I know I'll get the rest of the story later, but in this moment, I move toward my son and wrap my arms around him.

"You said you would find justice for her, and you did." I look into his tear-filled eyes. "Susannah?" I ask again, shocked at this.

"The girls are going to be okay . . . there were three left."

Three girls left.

The words are so horrific.

* * *

It takes weeks for the whole story to come out, all the pieces to come together. When they do, things click into place in a way that horrifies me.

Susannah always wanted more children, so she found them. Turns out Terry was willing to do what Susannah asked, because she knew he'd been illegally selling drugs for years, and she promised to use it as blackmail. Besides, he wanted more children too; he was a devoted husband.

They used the information I gave them about where David and James were working to go after girls, thinking it would be a cover in case anything happened to one of them, if one of the girls got out or something leaked. Then they would try and pin it on David and James somehow, although it wouldn't have worked that well. It didn't matter anyway, because they covered their tracks incredibly well.

They found girls and kept them medicated, kept them locked up here as some sick game, some perverse family in which they felt like they were in control.

215

I tried to understand it; I did. What happened that made Susannah snap?

It turns out, ten years ago when she became friends with Lisa and me, that acted as the catalyst. She wanted more kids. We kept having them. She was jealous. So she found girls of her own, girl after girl.

Leah was never a part of the plan. Leah was in the wrong place at the wrong time, or maybe the right place at the right time. Josh and Susannah had been at her birthday party that night. She saw how much everyone loved Leah and wanted her for herself, so she told Terry after the party what he needed to do — go back for her. And he did.

He followed her, kidnapped her easily, brought her to their home late at night.

Nathan didn't know. Or if he did, he has been protected.

Josh and Susannah — Father and Mother — kept Leah locked up with the other girls.

Monsters in our own backyard, members of the community, our homeschool co-op. She was our best friend.

And now, she will be in prison for the rest of her life.

CHAPTER 42

Annie
Three months later

It's a beautiful day for a summer wedding. The middle of August, blue skies, bright sun, green grass. Everyone's smiling. Jubilee can't stop grinning, because her big brother, Elijah, is here on leave from the Army for the wedding.

Jubilee is a flower girl, and when she walks down the aisle, fluttering rose petals, everyone swoons. When Emily and Jaden stand at the altar to say, "I do," Pastor Craig marrying them, tears fill my eyes. I squeeze David's hand. How did we get so lucky?

After the wedding, Lisa finds me, and I give my best friend a hug.

"I am so glad you're here," I tell her.

"I wouldn't have missed it for the world," she says. "I've watched Emily grow up."

It is impossible to not feel a pang of heartache, knowing her daughter, Leah, will never have a day like this. A day like this with Josh. Lisa must be able to read my mind.

"I want you to know," she says, "and I know I've said it a hundred times, but you raised a good boy."

"Stop, Lisa," I say.

"You know I mean it," she says. "Without him, Leah would have never found justice."

I squeeze her hand. We look at the reception hall of the church. All of our friends and family are here. It's a beautiful wedding. Simple and romantic, flowers everywhere, Emily in her big white dress.

"It's still shocking, isn't it?" I ask. "The fact that Susannah's not a part of this day."

"I think I'll be shocked about it until the day I die," Lisa says.

It's crazy to imagine a woman we thought was our friend could be capable of such horror, and it makes you wonder how much you really know anybody.

I thought I knew Susannah, but then I realized that over the years of our friendship, she was always the one coming to me. She'd bring me extra food she cooked. She'd ask my mother-in-law, Sarah, for advice on canning or sewing. She'd come to co-op tired, and sometimes I wouldn't understand why, but now I realize she was taking care of four other girls — ultimately, five — not just Nathan.

And Nathan. Poor kid. He moved to his aunt and uncle's house in Idaho after his parents were arrested and put on trial.

They pleaded guilty to everything. The amount of evidence was so damning, there was no way they could deny a thing. Everything had been documented on camera for years.

The three surviving girls, Beth, Carrie and Lindy, were reunited with their families. It had been years that they'd been missing. The body of a fourth, Tamara, was found in a garbage bag in the back of their property. Apparently, Terry and Susannah thought that eventually it would just decompose, and no one would come looking.

It's horrific, all of it. I don't want to think about it on a day like today.

"I should have never brought it up," Lisa says, her thoughts mirroring mine.

"It's okay," I say. "Hopefully, one day, some of those images will fade from our minds."

But we both know that probably isn't true. They'll make a true crime documentary about this. There are so many photographs, so much footage, that it's unnerving. Susannah had been recording these girls the entire time they were locked in their basement.

I can't imagine being the parents of the girls and sifting through the footage, watching their children grow up before their very eyes in such a disturbing way. Lisa has told me about parts of what she has seen. As a mother of one of the victims, she's been privy to more details than anyone else.

"So," Lisa says, "now that the wedding's done, it's almost September, a new school year."

I look at her. "It'll be weird having co-op again without Susannah, won't it?"

Lisa clasps my hand in hers, squeezing it in a comforting way. "Hopefully there will be a new sense of peace, for everyone. And it will be a happy year for me, especially."

"Why is that?"

She smiles, looking down at her belly. "I'm twelve weeks pregnant."

"Oh, Lisa, congratulations," I say. But there are tears in my eyes, and I don't know why. There is a twinge of sorrow for how narrow my friend's life will remain, mixed with a longing for the life I never had at all.

It's complicated, motherhood. Our hearts are given over to the ones we raise, and it is easy to get lost.

Jubilee runs over to me, a glass of pink punch in hand, happiness written on her face.

But we don't always have to be lost. We can be found too.

I wrap Jubilee in a hug, knowing I won't be able to hold on forever, but today, I can. Today, I will.

THE END

THE JOFFE BOOKS STORY

We began in 2014 when Jasper agreed to publish his mum's much-rejected romance novel and it became a bestseller.

Since then we've grown into the largest independent publisher in the UK. We're extremely proud to publish some of the very best writers in the world, including Joy Ellis, Faith Martin, Caro Ramsay, Helen Forrester, Simon Brett and Robert Goddard. Everyone at Joffe Books loves reading and we never forget that it all begins with the magic of an author telling a story.

We are proud to publish talented first-time authors, as well as established writers whose books we love introducing to a new generation of readers.

We have been shortlisted for Independent Publisher of the Year at the British Book Awards three times, in 2020, 2021 and 2022, and for the Diversity and Inclusivity Award at the Independent Publishing Awards in 2022.

We built this company with your help, and we love to hear from you, so please email us about absolutely anything bookish at feedback@joffebooks.com

If you want to receive free books every Friday and hear about all our new releases, join our mailing list: www.joffebooks.com/contact

And when you tell your friends about us, just remember: it's pronounced Joffe as in coffee or toffee!

Milton Keynes UK
Ingram Content Group UK Ltd.
UKHW040022281223
435051UK00004B/102